Breaking Good

Breaking Good

Madeline Ash

TULE
PUBLISHING

Dedication

For my glorious grandmothers, Marian and Patti —
thank you both for reading my stories,
encouraging me, and not commenting on all the sex.

Prologue

H E WASN'T GOOD for her. He never would be.

But Stevie Case had come anyway. Driven by the intensity of the looks they shared in the corridors; looks that went for so long, her stomach knotted and her muscles bunched and his friends all turned to follow his gaze. Driven by the fantasy he embodied—a rebel, wild and gorgeous, a boy who never in a million reincarnations would consider commitment. Driven by his personal invitation, murmured as he passed too close behind her locker, 'Come to my going-away party. We can't end like this.'

They couldn't end with so much unspoken between them. So much untouched.

Stevie arrived late. Late enough the night was on the verge of becoming a very early morning.

She found him alone.

He was sitting on the front porch, his head resting back against a brick pillar, eyes closed and a beer bottle loose in his hand. The party's sole survivor, surrounded by empty bottles and cans, cigarette butts, and discarded pizza boxes. The outside bulb cast him in dingy light, catching the hair on his arms, the shadow beneath the cut of his jaw, and the metal of the defaced coin around his neck.

His foot moved. His usual restless tapping.

He hadn't noticed her.

They weren't friends. Didn't move in the same circles. They rarely spoke. But they looked, and God, did those looks say more than Stevie could have ever put into words.

She'd known him since primary school. He'd always been disengaged, distracted—the boy who'd arm wrestled her behind the teacher's back for weeks before realizing Stevie wasn't short for Steven; who'd then asked if she'd squeal if he hurt her, and when she'd shot back, 'No, will you?' he'd continued wrestling without gender bias or mercy.

Mercy still wasn't his strong suit, or he'd have invited her over years ago.

Cautious, she passed through the paint-chipped front gate, breath held, wondering how many of those bottles were his. When her shoe scuffed over a crack in the concrete path, his eyes snapped open, locking onto her. His attention pressed hard into the center of her chest, reviving her heart to a heightened state of life. Pounding, contracting, aching.

'Stevie,' he murmured, a slow smile waking his features.

'Hey.' She paused, uncertain, sliding an unsteady hand into her back pocket. An act to hide how completely he undid her. Composure came naturally to her, nothing forced or feigned, but one look from Ethan and her sturdy heart leapt and her stomach wrung and her thoughts tangled together like anxious fingers.

It drove her crazy.

'You made it.' He rose to his feet, and she took in well-worn jeans, black boots, and a dark T-shirt with longer sleeves rolled up beneath. Masculine, almost rough, if it weren't for the lingering cherub face of his childhood—enviably even skin, sweeping lashes, and tawny-tiger eyes. For years, Stevie had suspected those eyes were nature's warning sign, like red on a spider's back or the colored bands of a coral snake. Yellow eyes meant danger.

Stevie faked ease. 'You said to get here any time after four o'clock, right?'

'Yeah.' Amused, he leaned a shoulder against the bricks, idle, sexy. 'In the afternoon. Thought you'd prefer the barbeque to the party.'

She'd arrived late to catch his bluff. Surely he'd make it with another girl when she didn't show.

Apparently not.

'I'm vegetarian.' She raised a shoulder.

'I bought gourmet veggie delights.' His lips twitched.

'I don't know your friends.'

'I told them to be nice,' he said.

'I'm not into rap.' Even to her, it sounded like a question.

'I downloaded PJ Harvey. Told the guys they'd have to deal with it.'

She paused, frowning. 'How'd you know?'

He broke their stare, looking aside. 'You wore her shirt on a free dress day last year.'

Stevie's pulse glitched. 'Oh.'

'Your parents know you're out this late?' His eyes locked back on her.

'My foster parents,' she corrected. 'And no, they think I'm pulling an all-nighter. They're not into helping me prep for exams, so they won't be checking in.'

'I'll help.' Thoughtful, he ran a hand through his disordered hair. 'What's the name of your favorite movie?'

'*Donnie Darko.*' She smiled wryly. 'Which will no doubt be in my physics exam, thanks.'

'Hey, it's quantum.'

That was the thing about Ethan. He wasn't stupid. He just hated school. The teachers had given up on him in early high school, around the time he gave up on himself, abandoning his classroom disruptions in favor of disturbing his entire life. Skipping classes, drinking, working nights stocking shelves—which only meant more missed lessons. When at school, he hung out behind portables or at the edge of the property, and when he rocked up to class, it was without interest or textbooks. A shadow student—for even when present, he wasn't really there.

Theoretically, not Stevie's type.

Physically—everything she wanted.

Eyeing his mostly empty bottle, she asked, 'Drinking alone?'

He swirled the amber liquid. 'Calms me down.'

'Worried about moving away?'

His index finger drummed against the neck of the bottle as he held her gaze. 'There's that,' he said. 'Then there's the unknown quantity standing before me.'

Stevie mocked curiosity and glanced over her shoulder.

His lips curved. 'I didn't think you'd turn up. Once midnight rolled around, I figured it'd all been in my head—with a head like mine, that's more than likely.'

'Yet, you waited.'

'I couldn't think about anything else.' He swigged from the bottle, his hand trembling.

'Got the shakes?'

'Never been so nervous.'

Imagine how she felt. At least he knew this game. Stevie was playing blind. She shifted, swallowing, her own shaking hands still locked in her pockets.

His head tilted. 'I didn't think you were the shy type.'

'I'm not the random-hookup type.'

'Years in the making is hardly random, Stevie.' His eyelashes cast whiskered shadows over his cheeks as his attention dipped. 'You dressed up for me.'

Warmth curled around her middle. He'd noticed. She wore black skinny leg jeans and her favorite Elliot Smith band T-shirt, complete with a vest over the top. Her flat canvas shoes were graffitied with permanent marker and her short, blonde hair stuck out from under a plaid newsboy cap.

No heels, bare legs, or dress hugging whatever figure she usually hid under loose clothes, but it was sharp, slick, and carefully selected for the occasion.

Ethan's appreciative gaze had her skin tightening, nerve endings aching for his touch. 'No one else home?'

'My brother's at that warehouse party, and Mum's doing the graveyard shift.' Then he said, 'Your sister was here earlier.'

Regan. Willful, careless, and only sixteen. Too similar to Ethan—skipping school, partying, thoughtless of her grades or future. She was a constant source of anxiety balled up in Stevie's stomach. 'She okay?'

'She's not one for pacing her drinks, but we got pizza into her.' He spoke quietly. 'She was all right by the time she left—but she'd heard I was waiting for you and threatened a lifetime of pain if I went anywhere near you.'

'Teasing?'

'She got into specifics. Trust me. She meant it.'

Stevie frowned.

'I imagine, like the rest of us, she knows you're too good for me.'

A shadow slipped through Stevie's conscience, all too aware of their differences. She was smart, with plans to go to university and become a structural engineer—he had no plans and was moving away from Melbourne three weeks before final exams. He drank, he debauched, he drove too fast—she studied hard and used soccer to vent her energy.

He continued, voice growing rough. 'Another study question. If there's a magnetic force acting between opposite-ly charged bodies, an attraction pulling them together, do they have any choice but to connect?'

It sure as hell didn't feel like it.

'Depends on how close they get,' she murmured.

'Huh.' Ethan leaned down and set his bottle on the top step. He straightened, eyes finding hers, and something on his face seized her pulse and doubled it. They'd skirted around their attraction for years, but they knew. Had always known. Eye contact was too intimate, too close to mind reading for them not to be aware of their mutual sexual chemistry.

Extending his hand toward her, he asked, 'Will you come closer to me, Stevie?'

Nerves twisted her insides into wire, tight, hard.

She'd thought about this moment all week—tried to use the facts to convince herself it was a bad idea. Stevie's neighbor and closest friend Felix had done his best to help. 'He's leaving town. Nothing can happen between you two. Why knowingly turn down a dead-end road?'

Because it *was* a dead-end. Serious sexual chemistry didn't make a perfect match, but it could make a perfect moment, and she ached to be touched like she mattered. No one seemed to want a tomboy. Not when they couldn't see the size of her breasts or envision where their hand might rest on her waist. Most teenage guys made no secret of wanting a girl to be hot and cute and sweet, and Stevie couldn't stomach the idea of even pretending to be those things. But Ethan noticed her, and he wanted what he saw.

She'd come tonight knowing they weren't couple material. She'd disdain his lack of ambition. He'd resent her goals. They would be toxic together.

They were made to end.

And to end like this.

She took his hand, thrilled by the feel of his fingers closing around hers. Gently, deliberately, he guided her onto the porch beside him. For the space of a shaky breath, he waited, watching her, a silent warning of her last chance. Then his lips covered hers, hands sliding around her as if they'd done this a thousand times. She held still, enlivened by the leathery scent of him, the coarse stubble against her chin, the firm press of his palms at her back. His head tilted, lips easing apart, seeming to sense her nerves and leading the kiss so very carefully. Heat slithered to her core when he teased her tongue into his mouth, and fire sparked in her heart when he moaned, kissing her deeper. He kept it slow, savoring, building the tension in her body until she was grasping his back, drawing him closer, and he spun, pressing her spine against the brick pillar.

He sank against her, unrestrained, and their movements roughened. He dragged off her hat, burying his hands into her hair. She lifted a foot and planted the sole on the bricks behind her, inhaling raggedly when he grasped her raised knee, guiding it outward so his hips could press down against hers. A new tension wrung through her body, tightening her breasts, and she knew she wanted this…wanted more.

Ethan drew back, pressing his forehead to hers and catching his breath.

He said softly, 'Tell me why you're here.'

She swallowed and flicked a glance at his parted lips. 'Three guesses.'

'You want me. I want you.' Even his hot breath on her face made her ache for him. 'And I'm leaving in the morning.'

She stiffened at the accuracy of the last.

His features twisted, cynical. 'You can finally do this without consequences.'

No point lying. 'Okay. I like that school's almost over, so I don't have to deal with everyone who thinks this is their business.'

'What about the consequence of us getting into some kind of relationship?'

Some kind, she noted. Not exclusive or long term, but something messier, murkier. He was right—*some kind of relationship* was exactly what she'd been avoiding.

'Ethan.' She nudged a few bottles off the porch with her foot. 'We have nothing in common.'

'We've got one very fierce thing in common,' he corrected, tightening his hold. Her chest pressed up against his, and arousal opened inside her, a lush flower. 'But it's only okay to act on it now because there's no future in it.'

She stared him down. 'You invited me here, knowing you leave in the morning, so it clearly doesn't bother you *that* much.'

He looked aside. A hand rose to swipe over his chin, nudging emotion off his face. 'I wouldn't be good for you; we both know that,' he said quietly. 'Guess I just wish it weren't true.'

Wariness rose in her. Her feelings for Ethan confused her. For years, she'd desired him, ached for his attention, hoped every day to see him around school. She'd imagined them together, holding hands, walking to class, and—because she'd even gone so far as to imagine having a positive influence on him—studying together. But then, her head would pipe up, accusing her of knowing better.

Every time, her heart relented.

Of course she knew better.

'I guess I've been thinking about why I'm leaving,' he said, leg jiggling slightly. 'Trying to convince myself it's the right thing to do.'

'And?'

'Turns out it is.' He looked down at her. Maybe it was the result of a long, sleepless night, or maybe it was her, but his gaze bared all. Grim, agitated, with a blackness that hinted at despair. 'This life isn't for me. Suburbia. Institution. Routine. It's overwhelming in its banality, like a thousand boring voices all talking at the same time. Impossible mind noise. I can't focus. Or the good part of me can't, so the lowlife has taken over.'

She twisted a knuckle between his ribs. 'You're not a lowlife.'

Ethan huffed out a humorless laugh, edging away. 'That's nice of you, but I am. I've got to get out, or I'll never be better.'

The student in her couldn't help saying, 'Wait until after exams.'

'I've failed, Stevie.' His gaze was bleak. 'Failed it all. Mr. Jefferson told me a few weeks ago.'

She stared, dismayed. 'I'm sorry.'

'I've never been smart enough.'

'That's bull.' His interest was the problem, not his intelligence. But it was too late now. 'Where will you go?'

'No idea. But Beau'—his brother—'reckons I'm the only person in our family who has a hope of succeeding, and he's not going to let me throw that away by ending up like him.' He gave a halfhearted smile. 'I said his life looked good to me, and he told me to get a grip and punched me in the face. Strangely, that silenced the mind noise for a second, and I realized he was right.'

Stevie grimaced. Brotherly love came in all forms.

'I don't know what I'll do.' He exhaled hard. 'But I'll find something. Get on track. Make myself better.'

Stevie nodded, hiding a chill of premonition. By moving away with no family and no support, the odds were against him. Good habits were hard to make, and bad habits hard to shake. Her stomach dropped as his future all but materialized before her.

A better life wasn't in the cards for Ethan Rafters.

'Good luck,' she murmured, looking down.

His hands found her again, pressing along her waist, her back, drawing heat from her core and calling it forth to her skin. Her body sighed, and she leaned into him as he said, 'I want to become the kind of person you'd want to stay around.'

She frowned. 'I'm really not your type.'

'You define my type.' He lowered his lips to her neck and dragged them across her skin. Reaction zapped through her veins and throbbed hot between her thighs. He kissed the hollow behind her ear, sending shivers over her scalp. 'You're tough. You do whatever the hell you want, and you do it unapologetically. You're *you*, and not many people go through school as themselves.' His hold tightened, thrilling her hormones with a simple slide of his hand over her bottom. 'Your smile drives me wild. When you hang out with Felix, he makes you laugh.' Jealousy tinged his words. 'Some days, it travels across the oval. It's so infectious that sometimes the guys ask what I'm smiling about. Your outfits are sexy. And your hair—damn—it's the coolest thing.'

His attention shifted in the dimness, roaming over her blonde spikes. Stevie managed to haul in a half-breath before he locked eyes with her and reached out. Large, gentle, his hand spanned across her scalp. Warmth flooded her, chased by arousal, as his fingertips tightened, massaging slightly, and shivers rushed down her neck, her spine, mellowing her muscles.

Her inhale was ragged. The underside of his wrist rested against her cheekbone, his skin hot, and she gave in, pressing her lips to his pulse. The pad of his thumb stroked her temple, and she closed her eyes for several sweet heartbeats.

'I didn't want to leave without telling you the effect you have on me,' he said.

She opened her eyes, pained.

He smiled ironically. 'Too deep?'

'A little.'

A little too deep, because now she knew this went beyond attraction on his end. And she...she was blinded by infatuation. She didn't know what she'd think of him if she could see clearly. 'Ethan—'

'Do you want to go inside?' His murmur cut her off; cut them both off from the conversation.

Stevie pressed her forehead against his, knowing it was now or never, with sunrise spreading pale grey across the eastern sky. Finally surrendering to the physical pull that had commanded her for so long, she whispered, 'Yes.'

It was how they were made to end, after all.

Chapter One

'MUM, DO I have to go?

Stevie held down a groan as she rubbed sunblock over her arms. The beachside hotel room was bright with early morning light, glowing off white walls and wooden floors, flaring the sunflower yellow of the hammock that hung on the small balcony. In the three days they'd been in Bryon Bay, the constant crash and drag of the waves below had become a second heartbeat, and the salty water like a second skin. Their days had flowed lazily from late breakfasts to barefooted walks on porcelain sand; from water fights in the aqua sea to sun-induced napping under beach umbrellas.

Today pressed pause on such bliss. And Zach wasn't happy.

'Mum?' he pushed, sitting on the edge of his bed.

'Are we running lines?' She plucked her cap off the sideboard and tugged it over her short hair. 'Because you keep asking me that.'

'Only 'cause you keep getting the answer wrong.'

Not taking the bait, Stevie slung her bag over her shoulder. Overalls, brushes, and a drop sheet were all concealed by the fluffy towel on top.

Zach continued, not moving from the bed. 'You're supposed to say: *No, my darling boy, you don't have to go. And yes, you can have lemonade with breakfast.*'

'We've got different scripts.' Distractedly, she patted the pockets of her shorts and felt her wallet and phone. Okay, it was time to get moving. 'Because mine says, *Yes, you have to go. Now.*'

He waved a hand. 'Old version.'

Stevie's flat stare found his tawny eyes full of false innocence. For a moment, regret knocked her off balance. Of course she didn't want him to go. They should be spending every minute of this trip together, swimming, exploring, and eating themselves stupid. She certainly shouldn't be sending him to a holiday program while she snuck off behind his back.

He trusted her, her bold boy, as she trusted him. Zach was seven years old, smart, sensitive, and on the trying side of assertive. Definitely too protective, but that was her own fault for saying, '*We need to stick together, you and me,*' too often over the years. Her close friend Felix was the only exception, since he'd been there all along. Even Stevie's own sister had been lucky to pass his approval just days before— after being missing for eight years. As for men, past forays into dating proved that Zach's childhood wasn't the time. His foul moods had been followed by tears so heartbreaking she'd thrown the idea of romance into her *Maybe When He's Older* basket.

A very full basket, that one, but Zach was everything to her. The buoy in her heart, the light in her eyes. No man was worth his unhappiness. Nothing was.

Hence the lies. She hated deceiving him, but she could hardly confide that she couldn't afford this trip, along with the year ahead. It was Zach's first holiday away from Melbourne. He'd been talking about it for months: the beach, the town, the sightseeing. There'd been a moment as the plane took off, when he'd gripped her hand and she'd pretended not to see the glisten of nerves in his eyes, but then they'd landed, and his undisguised excitement made it all worthwhile.

So she had to work in Byron Bay to make it possible—that was between her and her bank balance.

Zach was still watching her, his white-blond hair stark against his summer tan. His skin browned quickly, evenly, a golden reminder that a whole lot of his genes weren't hers. His shoulders were hunched and his skinny arms crossed tight, as if the power of body language could thwart a mother's word.

She crossed her arms back. 'You're going.'

'It's not fair.' His sigh was explosive. 'Other kids get a second chance by asking their dad. You say no, and that's that.'

Stevie's eyes narrowed, disguising an old sadness that

came hand in hand with guilt. *Ethan.* A mess of a memory, that man. Always devastating her with too many feelings. Sweet longing, sorrow, and cutting regret. Not regret over sleeping with him, or falling pregnant. No, that had gifted her with a son, and if there was one thing she'd never regret, it was Zach. But not telling Ethan about Zach before he'd died—for that, she'd carry guilt-burdened heartache for the rest of her days.

'I taught you what hypocrite means, didn't I?' she asked softly.

Zach paused. 'Yes.'

'And?'

His posture slumped. 'I shouldn't complain about not having a dad, when I don't want a dad.'

'Makes sense, doesn't it?'

He looked away. 'But I want to hang out with you.'

'You always hang out with me. I'm going to read and sleep and unsubscribe from emails. You get to have fun.'

'But I won't know anyone.'

'It's a holiday program. No one knows anyone. And it's only for ten days.' When his look darkened, she said, 'We'll go to the skate park afterwards.'

'But I want to hang out with Auntie Regan. We have my whole life to catch up on.'

Her gaze flattened. 'You're really subtle at changing tack. We'll have dinner with Regan and Felix tonight.'

'You must want to spend time with her.'

Of course she did. Stevie had scarcely recovered from the shock of Regan's return. Having to work instead of clutch her sister's hand was an unwelcome dose of reality, but they had the rest of their lives to be together. She clung to that.

'Correct,' she said. 'And how does that help your case?'

He paused, said, 'But *Mum,*' and changed tack again. 'Can't I start tomorrow? I'm already late.'

Her stomach hitched as she rolled her eyes. That meant she was late, too. Great way to start a new job. 'Come on, Zach. Felix put a lot of thought into this Christmas present.' He'd believed it would give Zach new experiences and Stevie a real break. 'And today is the start of surfing lessons—you miss out, and you won't be able to teach me when it's over.'

His features lifted fractionally.

'Parker's downstairs.' A blond, golden-skinned local friend who surely had salt water for blood, such was his love of the sea. His partner Alexia was away on a retreat with her friend Dee, and Zach seemed to be providing a welcome distraction. Parker also happened to own this very hotel—Lullabar—and had granted Zach free use of the lemonade hose. Naturally, they were now best buds for life. 'He's waiting to walk to the clubhouse with you. That makes you an instant cool kid, arriving with one of the surfers.'

That clearly held appeal, because Zach stood and uncrossed his arms. He pushed one last time. 'Since you're sentencing me to abject misery at a school away from school, will you at least pick me up?'

Stevie tilted her head. This client had set a demanding work schedule, but she'd just have to say that leaving at four was nonnegotiable. She owed Zach that much.

'I will if you tell me what abject means,' she said, opening the door.

He glared at her, caught out.

She grinned, kicking him lightly out the door. 'I'll be there.'

ETHAN RAFTERS JOGGED up the sandy path that led to his beachside home, sweating hard. His brindled boxer, Hack, took off in front of him, panting heavily and making a beeline for his dog pool under the eaves. Ethan glanced at his watch as he climbed the steps to the first-floor balcony. He'd been running for an hour and thirty-four minutes.

Take that, restless energy.

Aside from his heavy breathing and pounding pulse, the morning was serene. His sprinkler system hissed softly in the garden beds below, cicadas chirped in the strappy gums growing tall on his property, and water crashed down on the beach. He'd miss those waves, the way they allowed him to ride high and fast with the sunrise, but batted him down like a mother's hand if he lost focus; the way they clung to his hair, salty and stiff, long after he'd scuffed home. He'd miss the pace, too, for physics prevented the sea from crashing beyond a certain speed. With a mind prone to sensory overstimulation, Ethan seriously appreciated that.

He kicked off his shoes and stripped his damp shirt over his head, draping it over the balcony railing. As he started stretching, he noticed his retired neighbors wave from their patio.

He raised a hand, nodding.

The couple had stopped commenting on his energy a while back. When he'd first moved in, they'd laughingly called him a health nut. Then he'd got stuck into the renovations, and their jokes had petered out. He'd landscaped the garden. Ripped out the carpet inside and polished the boards beneath. Refitted the kitchen and the bathroom. All the while, he poured himself into his business. It was vital he always had a physical task on the go, because at twenty-six, he'd disproven the notion that he'd '*grow out of it*' by still having a mind without an off button.

Ethan bent further over his leg, hamstring tightening. He was moving back to Sydney in a few weeks, because when he stayed still too long, he got bored. Edgy. Started reaching for entertainment better left untouched.

He'd learned that the hard way.

Rarely did he wish for a reason to stay in one place, but when he did, it came with a heightened buzzing in his head and an almighty ache at the base of his ribcage that took days and a series of strong drinks to dislodge. This morning, he'd awoken with a telltale tightening, the predictive stirrings of loss. A bad sign, meaning he'd need to fill the final few weeks with more distractions than he had already lined up.

Work. Preparing to leave. Helping out a friend for the last time. Repainting the house before he rented it out.

Due to a twist of fate, the latter had him checking his watch again.

A consequence of his overactive mind was an inability to focus on mundane tasks. Paying the bills. Checking emails. Writing a shopping list. And, as it turned out, scrolling through the profiles of painters registered to work in his region. On the brink of death by tedium, a name had leapt out at him like a streaker at a business conference.

Stevie Case. Licensed. Six years industry experience.

He'd done a double take. He'd assumed Stevie had become a civil engineer, building cities or bridges, striding around construction sites with a hard hat and the respect of her colleagues. But then, he'd enlarged her profile picture, and recognition had thumped him in the chest. No mistaking those steady brown eyes, the sweet shape of her mouth. His Stevie Case was seeking temporary work in Byron Bay? His thoughts had spilled over, running into the idea of seeing her again after all this time, chatting and catching up as they worked side by side. It would be just like woodwork class—except he'd actually work this time.

When he'd enquired about her availability via the disappointingly impersonal *Request Job* button, she'd accepted—even with the timeframe that demanded a start only two days after Christmas and no break until every room gleamed white, New Year's be damned. He needed the painting done, and she had no issue with that.

After eight years, he was going to see Stevie again.

A sudden knock echoed off the high ceilings and empty floors, sending Hack hurtling up to the balcony and through the open doors toward the front of the house. Ethan cursed, beset by a sudden squall of nerves, and darted up to the mezzanine to grab a fresh shirt. Then he was striding toward the front door, reminding himself they were adults now, different people, and he didn't have to worry about being overpowered by hormones as his present met his past.

Striving for casual, he opened up.

Stevie was screwing the lid back on a water bottle, face lowered. She could easily be mistaken for an apprentice, with that smooth-skinned jaw and lean, fresh-out-of-school arms. She wore a cap pulled low and appeared to have ambitions about growing into her extra-large overalls.

Instantly overwhelmed, Ethan's mind clicked through memories like hyperlinks. *Stevie—near-androgynous—fine featured—stubbornly set chin—clever—carrying textbooks— studying—so confident—soccer—muddy jersey over her head— brown eyes—always staring back—the agony of nothing to say—attraction fierce in his blood—high school—after school— wanting, wanting, wanting—having—leaving.*

Amazement pounded him anew.

Stevie was here.

He'd watched her once, longed for her, ordered himself to steer clear because she didn't deserve the likes of him. The girl whose stares had stripped him bare. Whose self-awareness disarmed him—for what social armor did one use against a complete lack of pretense? She'd been the purest thing he'd ever touched, flaring in the shadows of his adolescence.

'Hey, Stevie.'

Her gaze sharpened on his, perplexed, and his focus narrowed, blocking out everything but the woman in front of him. For a few blissful heartbeats, the buzzing in his head stopped, and it was just silence.

Silence and Stevie.

Then recognition flashed across her face, followed by horror, and his thoughts exploded in a million directions.

THAT VOICE HIT her like ice water. She reeled at the way he said her name, familiar, warm, and softly intimate—way too intimate. Immobilized, Stevie stared into eyes she'd once sought daily; an intense stare that used to hook low inside her and tug—just like this—but no, that wasn't possible, so this, this man—must be dreaming. She must be dreaming. Stuck in a new nightmare, another that would leave her heaving with grief, gasping from the knife that couldn't be pulled from her past.

She breathed in. Out.

The next breath stabbed her lungs, sharp from the run uphill, and it came with the heady smell of brine and damp soil. The summer sun tore harshly at the back of her neck and glared into her eyes. Her head pounded; her stomach clenched.

All too real for a dream.

'I'm here to paint,' she said, voice small with confusion.

'Yeah,' he said, and then gestured toward himself. 'It's Ethan. From school.'

Frightened, heart pounding, she stepped back.

Uncanny how closely he resembled how Ethan *would* look built like a man. Lean and sculpted and tall. The fawn of his hair darker, matching the short growth along his jaw. His skin a healthy bronze, striking against black shorts and a V-neck tee. No torn denim to be seen, but an old coin hung from his neck, and a dog sat curiously by his side.

'I'm the painter,' she whispered, not comprehending.

'I know, Stevie.' The man frowned. 'I think I've scared you.'

The thin plastic of her water bottle buckled in her grip. That wasn't Ethan.

It couldn't be.

'Are you okay?' His frown grew heavier. 'You're really pale.'

'And you're dead.' The words came out strangled.

He flinched.

Swallowing horror, she shook her head. 'This isn't possible.'

'Hey.' Wary now, he raised his palms. 'It's okay. I'm not

dead—never was. This is just a bit random.'

Random? *No.* Random meant there'd been a chance of this happening, no matter how unlikely. But this was ice-in-hell impossible.

'Six years ago,' she whispered into the hot summer morning. 'Ethan died.'

The man stiffened. His leg started jiggling, an unusual habit for a grown man. 'What?'

Not easy to think back while numb with shock, but she got there. 'Felix told me.' He'd attended the same university as a girl from their high school. To fill the awkward silence in the library queue, she'd told him about Ethan's recent death. Casual, life-destroying chitchat. 'Said Ethan collapsed at a rave. Took the wrong kind of pill and died before the ambulance arrived.'

It had sounded right. Distressing and tragic, but within the realms of possibility.

The man's whole bearing gathered in on itself. Detached, he said, 'That was my brother.'

Oh, Jesus.

This *was* Ethan.

The malicious powers of the universe had her misinformed. One piece of gossip had opened up a sinkhole that she'd been struggling to get out of ever since. Now with that gossip disproved, a new sinkhole was widening beneath her.

Way bigger than the first.

'I am so, so sorry,' she whispered.

'We were one and the same to most people.' Ethan's attention followed the hand she raised to the base of her neck, covering her stuttering pulse. 'You really don't look okay.'

'I'm—fine.' She was sinking fast.

'You're not. I've spooked you. Sorry. I thought it'd be fun.'

'Fun.' As she sank, guilt pumped into her veins, her muscles, gushed deep down into her chest. She thought of Zach, her brightest light turned darkest secret. She thought back to dropping him off this morning, and the way he'd turned to her with those clever kid eyes and said, '*Love you*,' because that was always the last thing they said to each other. And how she'd said it back, as always, taking it for granted because she'd been running late.

But Ethan couldn't take his son for granted. He couldn't be told by Zach that he was loved every morning, because he didn't know.

He didn't know.

Oh, God.

Sweet, merciful God, forgive her.

'Come in,' he said, standing back, concern clear on his face. 'It's cooler inside.'

Stevie eyed the open doorway. Inside was a world where Zach's father wasn't a memory, but a living, breathing, feeling man—a world unknown, unchartered.

Hands fisted, she forced each step, moving around him, unprepared for the pull of his body. Despite everything, it was magnetic, tight, grasping her like the sex-crazed hands in her memory. That night flashed back, a visceral reminder of a cautious kiss turned greedy. The hot slide of meeting bodies, desire flaring in the darkness, and the hot clutch of pleasure.

Stevie's pulse spiked.

Ethan leaned closer as he shut the door, his scent rushing into the hollow of memory. Light, masculine, leathery—for years, she'd sought that blend, and not even in her dreams had she found it.

Ethan's gaze was waiting for her, a honey-colored stare so sticky she knew she'd feel it on her skin for days. It dripped into her blood, thickening her pulse and turning her muscles to syrup. Eight years on, he was still the master of her desire.

Her next inhale was jagged.

'I'll get you some water.' His eyes flicked fast as fire over her figure. 'Hack, heel.'

Focus on the house, she ordered herself as she followed man and dog. *Don't think.*

The house. A contemporary construction with masonry and timber cladding, set into the slope of the hillside and surrounded by strappy plants and tropical trees. Modern, inside and out, with this grand entranceway and seamless skylights opening up the high ceiling.

The main living space was at the rear. Stevie halted in the threshold, dismayed by the magnificence of it, even with bare walls and plastic drop sheets covering the empty hardwood floors. Glass panels made up the entire far wall, currently folded aside to give unrestricted access to a balcony and the pristine beachside views beyond. A glass roof rose up like the sky above them, flooding the room with natural light. The entire house was white, bright, and beautiful.

And it was Ethan's.

'Is the fresh air good? I'll turn up the cooling,' he said, moving toward a sleek kitchen island. 'Please, sit down.'

Stevie and the dog both sat on the plastic-covered floor. Stunned, she remembered his mission to make himself a better person, and wretchedly, she realized she'd been less shocked by him dying of an overdose than she was now, faced with his obvious success.

Culpability tore her heart out.

She'd be better off without it, considering.

'Here.' He was passing her a glass of ice water. 'Drink.'

She drank. It ran cold into the new cavity in her chest.

He disappeared, and the flow of the air conditioner intensified. Then he was back, standing beside his dog with two connected wire loops in his hand. Without looking down, he slid the loops around, trying to untangle them. After a moment, he shook his head with a rueful smile. 'Sorry I scared you.'

A muscle slid in Stevie's jaw, holding back a breakdown. The right to fall to pieces was Ethan's, whether he knew it yet or not. Her right was to hold it together, and then figure out what the hell to do when she had the capacity to process this.

So she said, 'No problem,' and raised the glass again.

He broke into a laugh, soft and rolling, and she shivered at the sound. It was like listening to the future—Zach's laugh in twenty or so years. 'I've wanted to see you again.'

Surprise had the water sloshing against her upper lip.

'I saw your profile online.' His voice was warm. 'I couldn't really believe it.'

She lowered the glass and spoke around the lump in her throat. 'I can imagine.'

'I thought you studied engineering.'

'Not in the end.'

'But you worked so hard at school.' Not disappointment in those words, but curiosity.

Her voice was strained as she answered, 'I've worked hard since.'

'I'm sure of it.' Those eyes watched her. He didn't spare a glance down as his hands continued to manipulate the wire. 'You haven't changed a bit.'

Stricken, she stared back.

'Except for the panic,' he said after a moment, frowning. 'That's new.'

'I'm talking to a ghost. Wouldn't you panic?'

'Will it help if I promise not to haunt you?'

His memory had lurked in her conscience for a long time: gorgeous, foolish, wild. Softly, she said, 'I don't think that's up to you.'

His frown didn't ease.

Shifting the focus, she said, 'The panic's residual. I've had a big few days. Regan ran away from home a few weeks after you left.' Months before Stevie realized she was pregnant. A series of cruelly timed events. 'She came back again this Christmas Eve, actually. I'm still reeling.'

He nodded, his expression a mix of interest and incredulity. 'Wow.' At her stare, he smiled. 'I've really wanted to see you again.'

Her gut wrenched. 'So you own this place?'

He hesitated, seeming confused by her lack of shared enthusiasm. 'Yeah. But I'm about to rent it out. Work is taking me to Sydney.'

She raised a brow, hoping it was a clear enough question.

'A new adventure,' he said. 'I'm handing over control of my business to work on a community side project.'

'What's your business?' she asked, desperate to keep the spotlight on him.

'A plastic-wood composite company—it's a timber alternative.'

'And the side project?'

'I've been approached to contribute to a community program in Indonesia. We're going to clean up the plastic litter in the area, and then turn it into plastic-wood composite for community housing.' He paused, and the two loops of wire came apart. He tossed them onto the kitchen bench. 'We'll be working with the government-housing department and relief-funding agencies. It's really exciting.'

Her lungs faltered.

With a soft smile, he said, 'I told you I was going to make myself better.'

She lowered her face. If guilt could kill, she'd be splattering these walls.

He asked, 'So what have you been up to all this time?'

Raising your child.

Panic flared in her gut. *No.* Shit. *No, no.* She couldn't do this now.

She gestured around the room, arm jerking. 'Where should I start?'

He paused at the shutdown. 'Stevie. What's wrong?'

She didn't answer. Kept her eyes on the walls. The big, rich-person walls. Void of furniture, she realized there were no signs of whether Ethan had a partner, a family, loved ones who would also be affected by this. Horrified, she asked, 'Are you single?'

A startled pause. 'That's what's bothering you?'

She didn't answer; didn't look at him.

'Yes, I am,' he said, voice confused. 'Though I've never heard that question sound so fraught. I don't suppose you're asking me out?'

'No.' She put down the water glass and quickly lied. 'Just like to know who else might be coming in and out while I'm working.'

'No one else.' Ethan shifted. Without even looking, she

felt the movement prickle across her skin, left to right. God, she was too aware of him. 'You know, if I thought you'd been dead all this time, I'd have been shocked to see you too. But relief would be kicking in by now. Maybe a smile. Or something.'

'You're on a deadline,' she managed to say. 'So I should get started.'

'Why are you unhappy to see me?'

Wordless, she looked back at him.

'You've always been a good memory for me.' His frown deepened. 'I'm not one for you.'

Her chest constricted. She couldn't tell him why. Not all of a sudden, not like this.

'I wouldn't have had you come here if I'd known.' He exhaled roughly. 'I thought it'd been good between us. I mean, you wanted to sleep with me. Didn't you?' His face paled. 'Christ, did I make that up in my head?'

'I wanted to.' *More than anything.*

'Then, why are you—' He started to pace as he gestured toward her. 'Do you resent that I left afterwards?'

Oh, the layers beneath that question. She resented he hadn't tried to contact her in the months that followed. She resented he hadn't told his family where he was going, effectively preventing her from contacting him. More than anything, she resented her gut feeling that he wouldn't succeed and the consequent decision to give up the search as she entered her third trimester, believing she and her baby would be better off without him.

His supposed death had justified her decision. A pill-popping partygoer wouldn't have been a responsible role model, nor would he have provided a stable home for her child.

But he hadn't died. He'd hauled himself into a better life.

Her resentment compounded. Larger than ever, it turned on her and attacked.

Ethan had succeeded. It was her own financial failures that had brought her to his doorstep, seeking his money to help support her son.

Their son.

'Ethan,' she managed, faint with self-disgust. 'I'm having a bad day.'

'But you knew I was leaving.' He stopped pacing and looked at her. 'I don't understand.'

'Please.' She couldn't hold it together much longer. 'Can we do this later?'

'I'm going to get stuck on it.' The intensity in his eyes confirmed that. 'Is it—do you want to call off this job? I don't want you hating every minute—'

'No.'

After a moment, he nodded. 'The equipment and paint is in the garage. Ignore all the boxes. That's stuff I haven't sent to Sydney yet. I'll help paint, just not today or tomorrow. I've agreed to help a friend with something.'

Thank God.

'I have to leave at four,' she said woodenly.

'That's fine.' He sounded resigned. 'Hack, stay.'

The dog stayed still, watching as Ethan moved onto the balcony, shucked a pair of shoes, and tugged a beach towel from where it hung over the railing. Then he poked his head back inside and said, 'I'm sorry I've upset you,' with such sincerity that Stevie's heart rent. She looked down, feigning disinterest.

She gave a nod.

After a heavy silence, she heard his footsteps retreat down a set of stairs off the balcony. The crunch of feet on dried leaves faded away toward the beach. Then, he was gone.

She curled in on herself. When her breath came faster, panicked, Hack bullied his way into her space, panting excitedly and ending up with Stevie's arms around his neck.

'Tell him for me,' she said as the dog licked her face. 'Please. I can't do it.'

When he made no promises, she battled to haul her breathing under control, to ease the squeeze of her lungs, because tomorrow, she knew she'd have to be strong.

Her choices had formed a canker in her conscience the moment she'd believed Ethan dead. She'd intended to track him down—but later, when life wasn't so chaotic and messed up, her sanity not hinging on what minimal stability she and Zach had. Then Ethan had died, and she'd been stuck with no way of rewriting the past. For years, she'd lived with that wrong.

Now, she'd have to make it right.

Chapter Two

ETHAN SET OFF along the beach, racing as fast as the thoughts in his head.

It had been eight years since he'd left home, well practiced at wasting time and dreaming without doing, but completely clueless when it came to anything resembling life skills. Eight years of struggling, learning, and forming ways to keep his shit sorted. And eight long years in which he hadn't felt even half as connected to anyone as he had to Stevie Case.

He slowed under the brunt of the sun's midsummer burn. He hung the towel around his neck, tugged it up to his nape, and pulled the brim of his cap low. The shade did nothing to ease the sting of Stevie's reaction to seeing him again, but he ran on.

Horrified. Floored. Alarmed. Not exactly the warm welcome he'd imagined, but she thought he'd died, and that kind of mental dislocation required time to set right. He hoped she'd have her head around it by this afternoon.

Then she could tell him what she was doing in Byron Bay. How long she'd been here, how long she was staying.

Maybe they'd lived in the same town since he'd moved in. Had he jogged passed her along the beach and not known to look? Had he surfed right beside her in the waves? That she exercised was obvious—no mistaking the fitness of her narrow frame. Her arms were well formed with muscle, lean and latent beneath the soft contours of her female skin. Her bearing had been sturdy, resilient, even in shock. If she was anything like she used to be, she knew how to handle herself. Was she still like that?

He had other questions. Questions he couldn't politely ask, and they snapped at him like sharks.

Was she married, committed, in love? Happy? Was she still attracted to him, or had he imagined that crackle in the air?

The house painting surprised him. But it fit—she'd always been active. Taken sport and technology classes, always played soccer, and then there'd been the semester in high school she'd made bets on winning wrestling matches. Not arm wrestles, but full-body grapples, and in the majority of cases, she'd pinned the guys and headed back to class with both their dignity and cash in hand. Ethan had watched on, silent, his thrumming masculinity desperate to challenge her, but he'd known that no matter who pinned whom, she'd have felt his attraction hard and sure between them.

It'd be no different now.

Never before had he found overalls so sexy, but along with her white singlet and work boots, she'd let lust loose inside him. The tantalizing contrast between the shapeless overalls and the fitted singlet, along with the unknown reality of whether a quick unclip of the straps would have the whole deal collapsing around a pair of bare legs—*legs—tight around him—desperate tangling—renewed lust—curiosity—slow this time—without urgency—tasting—pushing—building—dragging it out until her throaty moans became gasps, and she begged—*

Christ. *Cool your head, man.*

Beyond frustrated, Ethan slowed to a walk.

It had always been about imagination with Stevie. Not what there was, but what there might be. The kind of guessing game that had driven him mad in his youth, because he'd known no matter what was under those clothes, he wanted it to himself. A soft stomach or a taut set of abs, flat breasts or full, curvy hips or narrow, he'd stroke them, cup them, and devour them just the same. Whatever she looked like, he'd wanted it with every hot-blooded fiber of his being.

For one night, he'd had it.

And spent every night since wanting.

Enough. She was likely off-limits in one way or another. Working himself into a sweat wouldn't change that.

Time to focus on the task at hand. Scanning the crowded beach ahead, he noted a group of kids in wetsuits and neon zinc. They stood beside surfboards laid flat on the sand, shifting and squinting as they watched their instructor demonstrate how to balance. Their instructor was Vikas.

37

Ethan grinned as his friend bent at the knees, raising a hand above his head and lowering it in a straight line to the center of his chest, indicating internal balance.

For an unfathomably busy man, Vik always emanated an unreasonable level of calm. He owned a vinyasa yoga retreat outside of town that had a perpetual three-month waiting list; was always volunteering at local events; and ran this holiday program every quarter. Add to that, he was the father of three crazily beautiful children, all under age ten.

Vik claimed his calm was a part of his 'yogic presence'.

Ethan claimed Vik was capable of time travel and exploited the ability so regular non-time-travelling humans would be impressed by his generosity and time-management skills.

Vik told him to stop being ridiculous. Ethan told him to share the power of time travel.

Needless to say, they were at an impasse.

'And here's Ethan,' Vik told the group loudly, flashing him a wide smile. 'Right on time.' His tone added *not*. 'Now we can get in the water!'

The kids gave a small cheer, muted by a palpable sense of fear.

'Hey, relax, you guys,' Parker said, giving Ethan a friendly nod. 'Stick to paddling, if you'd prefer.' Parker was another of the instructors—a local surfer who had volunteered to help because his partner was expecting a baby. Apparently, teaching primary school kids how to surf was the equivalent to a crash course in parenting. 'Zach, want to lead the way, mate?'

A skinny blond kid picked up his board and moved with Parker into the water. Before long, the group was lined up and paddling haphazardly toward the shore. Ethan followed his friend's directive and stood waist deep in the waves, making sure no one drifted too far out. It kept him occupied enough, as did cooking at the barbeque for lunch, but once they'd all returned to the sea for the afternoon, Stevie strode back into his head and stopped front and center, hands toying with the metal clips on her overalls, tilting her head and not giving an inch.

He'd always been able to hyperfocus on Stevie.

'You've stopped blinking,' Vik murmured to him, facing the class but wading closer.

Ethan grimaced. 'Just distracted.'

'Usually your version of distracted involves involuntary tapping.'

'You can't see my feet.' He turned his face aside as a kid kicked hard toward the shore, splashing up a storm. 'The painter's a woman.' He lowered his voice. 'I've slept with her.'

Startled, Vik said, 'No wonder you were late.'

He smiled wryly. 'Not today. Years ago, back in high school.'

'Yeah? Small world.' His friend lunged sideways, grabbing a girl's board and spinning it toward the sand. After reminding her when to bring her knees up, he pushed her on her way. 'So is it good or not good to see her again?'

'Good for me. But I don't think it's good for—'

'You two want to stop gossiping and help me turn this thing around?'

Ethan glanced to his right. The blond boy whose name he already couldn't remember was paddling on the spot, struggling to get the board's nose facing the shore.

'Sorry, man.' He reached out and cranked it around. 'Use one arm to turn.'

'Oh.' The kid took off.

'We should haul them in now, actually,' Vik said, glancing at his watch. Then he raised a brow. 'We'll get back to this ex of yours.'

Twenty minutes later, the group had awkwardly removed their provided wetsuits and been revved up for tomorrow's class. After they scattered, Vik and Parker spoke to curious parents, and Ethan started carrying the boards and wetsuits back to the surf clubhouse. On his third trip, he noticed the skinny blond boy sitting on the sand, arms around his knees, glancing up and down the beach.

With the remaining boards tucked under his arm, Ethan moved closer. 'How'd you go today, mate?'

The boy glanced at him, golden-brown eyes catching him in the chest. 'I stood up. Then I fell off.'

'No one stands forever.'

'Wouldn't matter if I did,' the boy said, turning away to

set his chin on his knees. 'No one would see, anyway.'

'Pretty sure I heard Parker cheering you on like a madman.'

'Aside from him. My friends aren't here. My mum's not here.'

Ethan shielded his eyes with a hand. He'd spent years in school holiday programs and after-school care. He understood now how hard his mum had worked to keep food in the fridge and clothes in the wardrobe—he'd since repaid her tenfold—but back then, he'd resented her for not being around.

'You a local?' Ethan shifted so his feet sank beneath the hot surface of the sand.

'Nope. On a holiday.'

Which meant his mum wouldn't be working. Ethan kept a frown from his face. 'You here 'cause your mum's doing boring adult stuff?'

The kid's glare told Ethan he was aiming too young with his conversation. 'She's having a break. Without me.'

Right. Poor guy.

'If you have a phone, I can take a photo of you surfing tomorrow. You can show her after.'

The kid's face lit up. 'Could you?'

Ethan smiled. 'Yeah, easy.'

'Then she'll feel bad she wasn't here to see it.'

Ah. That would make Ethan an accomplice in a guilt-trip. Probably not what Vik meant when he'd said to help out. He extended his hand, trying to up the maturity scale. 'I'm Ethan, by the way.'

'Yeah, Vikas said so when you were late.' He slid Ethan a curious look and decided to shake. 'I'm Zach.' There was an awkward moment where Zach extended his left hand, only to realize that Ethan had offered his right, and they both went to swap at the same time.

'Go left.' Ethan grinned. 'I'm a leftie, too. Usually shake with my right so I don't confuse people.'

'Mum's told me not to change myself to suit others.'

'Good advice.' Zach's hand was little in his, almost delicate. Nothing like his attitude. Then his elbow rose as he did his best to squeeze Ethan's hand as hard as he could.

That was more like it.

'You don't have to wait with me.' The boy's hand went back to circling his knees. 'Mum won't feel as bad about being late if I'm waiting with someone.'

His brows rose. Yeah, this kid was definitely hurting. Ethan couldn't deny thinking similarly at his age. 'Catch you tomorrow, then.'

'Yeah. Oh—hey, can I ask you something?'

'Shoot.' He adjusted the boards under his arms.

Zach squinted up at him. 'What does abject mean?'

Frowning, he asked, 'As in abject suffering?'

'Yeah.' The boy shrugged. 'Or misery.'

Puzzled, Ethan said, 'Pretty sure it means really bad. Hopeless to the extreme. Misery is awful enough, but abject misery—you don't want it.'

'Huh.' Zach looked disappointed.

'Why?'

'I told Mum this program would be abject misery. No wonder I had to come. She won't let me win arguments by exaggerating. Or using words I don't understand.'

'Double whammy,' Ethan said in sympathy.

'Brutal,' the kid agreed.

'And was today miserable?'

Zach exhaled and shot him a look of amused surrender. 'Nah. But if I tell Mum, I'll be in an abject state of I-told-you-so.'

Ethan snorted.

'Anyway, shove off before she gets here.' But Zach smiled after he said it.

Amazed by his audacity, Ethan met Parker's eye across the sand. A silent exchange said the other man would stick around until Zach's mother arrived.

With that, thoughts of Stevie booted the kid clean out of his head. It was ten past four. Maybe he could catch her before she left, and maybe she'd feel more like talking.

And maybe, just maybe, he could find out if their attraction was still mutual.

ETHAN FOUND STEVIE kneeling in his front hall, jamming her work boots into a bag, overalls and a beach towel strewn on the floor beside her. Her head snapped up as he walked in, face blanching, and he ignored the squeeze in his chest. Evidently, hours of knowing he lived couldn't overwrite years of believing him dead.

'Hey,' he said, closing the front door behind him.

'Hi.' Voice wary, face down. She'd changed into knee-length denim shorts and flip-flops, and nailed hot casual in that white singlet. 'I'm almost out of here.'

'No rush.' Shoulder blades against the door, he watched her. 'Feeling any better?'

Her brown gaze flung to him as she rolled up her overalls. Her nod was unconvincing.

'You were going to tell me why you were upset.'

'Not running twenty minutes late, I wasn't.'

'Running a little late won't hurt you.'

Another glance, a little on the dry side. 'Not me I'm worried about.'

'You got a date?'

Overalls in, she crammed the beach towel on top and sprung to her feet. 'No.' But she strode toward him like she'd kick him aside if he didn't move, so move he did, leaning a shoulder just shy of the doorjamb, hands in his back pockets. He turned inwards as she reached for the door handle, a light gust traveling over him, soft like naked skin, heady like pheromones in action.

'See you,' he murmured as chemistry seized him.

So close—smart—short—his breath moved her hair—

beautiful—different with that reserved maturity—not different enough—his heart still hammered—was she single—interested—had she met her soul mate—swans mated for life—he wished he could—no one seemed to wish the same—she'd known half of his failures—total screw up—had wanted him anyway—could she want the rest—he wanted her to want it—he wanted to kiss her—all of it—right now.

Stevie had faltered, fingers gripping the door handle, and she watched him in a kind of cautious captivation. 'God,' she murmured. 'I'd almost forgotten that look.'

He held still. 'Tell me what I did to hurt you.'

She stood close enough that he could see paint dust in her blonde hair, far enough the distance killed him. 'Tomorrow.'

So he had done something.

Ethan took a chance. 'I want to be honest, because I wasn't back then.'

'I'm really running late.' But she didn't move. Stuck beside him, magnets locked together.

'I'm sorry I didn't contact you.' If he spat the truth out now, he wouldn't have to chew on it all night. 'I was a fool, and, in a weird way, it proves that I was right to leave. Because even when I was set on making myself better, I didn't take your number, didn't ask whether you'd want to work something out once I got my life on track. I slept with you and drove off into the sunrise like a selfish arsehole.'

She stared at him. Eyes wide, lips pinched.

'It was poor form, and I'm sorry,' he finished.

Features torn, her gaze fell to his chest. His skin tensed, one hundred percent willing for her to turn looking into touching. This wasn't nostalgia playing tricks. This was real. Sexual attraction as he'd only known it once before—*stares in the corridor—the smart girl—no-go zone—desperation—that one night—hot, forbidden release.*

'Do you ever think about that night?' His voice grew rough.

The truth was dark in her eyes as she looked back up at him. 'Sometimes.'

'In what kind of way?'

She hesitated. Her hand still clutched the door handle. 'A sad way.'

'Because you thought I was dead.'

She regarded him silently. Then, softly, 'But you weren't. All this time.'

'No.' He shifted closer, desire charging the space between them. She murmured, 'Ethan,' the kind of halfhearted protest that accompanied giving in, so he didn't touch, but didn't retreat, relying on the intensity of his awareness to log every humming inch of her body close to his.

Her breath caught. His pulse stuttered.

'Have you ever wanted that night over again?' The house was silent around them, inviting. Too easy to envision sun-drenched afternoon sex, daylight casting a raw edge onto their passion, exposed skin and straining bodies, her face lighting up as she broke beneath him. Because she would break, no easier promise, with this attraction spurring them on.

'Have you?' he pushed from low in his throat. No mistaking his real question. *Shall we?*

'We've as good as just met, Ethan. You don't know what you're asking.'

Belatedly, foolishly, he asked, 'Do you have a boyfriend? Or a husband or girlfriend or lover, or someone who means I need to back the hell away right now?'

Something strange flickered across her face as she resettled the bag strap. 'No.'

'Do you want one?'

She gave a half-nod, half-shrug. 'Who doesn't?'

'Which one?'

Her brows rose. 'I'm only allowed to want one?'

He ached to be more than one for her, just as he burned to kiss her, right here and now. 'I was attracted to you back then, but I wasn't right for you. Things are different now.' He shifted, the already-limited space between them falling away. His knuckles grazed the denim on her thigh, and he balled his hand to stop from spreading his fingers up and under the fabric.

Lust softened her features and loosened her jaw, her posture. But her stare held steady as she murmured, 'I have wanted that night again.'

His face dipped lower. He could see the flush on her cheeks; could feel the heat of her skin radiating against his.

He could almost taste her mouth. 'What are you doing tonight?'

She swallowed and hovered on the brink, breath hot, body painfully close to his. 'Not that.'

'Tomorrow night?' He wasn't ready to pull back. 'Let's go away for a few days. Screw the painting.'

'Ethan.' She peeled herself away from tension's stronghold, frowning at his impulsiveness.

'I've changed, if that's what this is about. Don't judge me now by my actions when I was eighteen.'

The frown remained. 'How would you be different?'

'What?'

'If we were to relive that night, how would you be different from when you were eighteen?' Something bitter twisted in her eyes. 'Because this is a working holiday for me. I'm visiting friends. I'll be back in Melbourne in two and a half weeks. As you said, you'll be in Sydney. How could you possibly think it could be different this time around, when you're already asking me to bed? I'm older now. I need more than attraction for that to happen.' Again, she asked, 'So how would it be different?'

He had no answer. Damn it. But it would be different. It had to be.

Her breath was coming fast, shaky.

'How can any of this possibly work?' Her voice broke. She ran a hand over her face as she turned away. 'I have to go,' she muttered, yanking the door open.

'Will you be back?' he asked quickly.

She cursed as she stepped outside, muttered 'Tomorrow,' and drew the door shut behind her.

Ethan was left alone, tortured by her questions and the lingering trace of her in the air.

AFTER TAKING ZACH to the skate park, Stevie spent the evening with him, Felix, and Regan in the surfie-grunge bar that made up the ground floor of Lullabar. She and Zach had declared their love for the venue upon arrival. The theme paid tribute to Parker's second company, surf brand Lullabyron. Old surfboards made up the bar surface, and neon graffiti messed up the charcoal-grey walls, glowing under ultraviolet lights. Industrial-sized fans blew from high up the walls, churning the sultry, sea-sticky air. The only softness in the bar's otherwise trendy edge was the cat basket sitting beside the counter, occupied by a white fluff ball that ignored all patrons so completely that Stevie suspected it was a miracle she tolerated Zach's daily cuddling.

He'd never had a pet.

The bar's rules allowed Zach downstairs under supervision except late on Thursday through to Saturday nights, when live music dominated—along with a steadier flow of booze and consequent adult content. Zach had cried discrimination. Stevie had offered to coat him in manure to help him grow up.

Thankfully, it was a Monday. One less battle to fight.

Zach had carried the limp and unwilling cat across to their booth, keeping her on his lap with the sheer force of childish ignorance. Sitting beside him, Stevie tried her best to act normal. She ate pizza. Ordered a second drink. She faked interest in Felix and Regan's recounts of their tandem hang-gliding flights, and she concealed the guilt embedded hilt-deep in her chest when Zach spoke about learning to surf 'by myself'. She even contributed, claiming she'd read the day away only to fall asleep late afternoon. But despite her best efforts, Felix still ended up eyeing her across the table in equal parts suspicion and concern.

He'd known her almost all her life. No doubt he could sense the emotional gunk hanging off her thoughts. Filling her heart. Obstructing her lungs.

Damn it, she couldn't get a clean breath.

'You promised to pick me up, and then you fell asleep,' Zach muttered darkly beside her.

Stevie counted to three before responding. Her voice wavered anyway. 'I hadn't planned on it.'

She hadn't planned on shock impacting her sanding speed and having to work late to prove to Ethan that she was worth paying.

'So not planning on it is a valid excuse now?' Zach asked sarcastically. 'I'll have to remember that next time you get me in trouble for, like, anything.'

'Knock it off,' Felix said from across the booth. 'Give

your mum a break.'

'That's just it.' Zach crossed his arms. 'She's taking a break without me.'

And that was when the gunk made it to Stevie's eyes. They filled with tears, and she gasped once, loudly, before locking her jaw and pushing out of the booth. She shouldered through the crowd and into the bathroom, ending up sitting on a closed toilet with her face pressed into her hands.

Shit.

She dragged in a breath. It cut at the base of her neck.

Oh, God.

Hot tears landed on the grey tiles. Breathing fast, way too fast, she squeezed her eyes shut.

What the hell was she going to do? *Tell Ethan*, she'd ordered herself earlier. *Just say it.* Don't think about the consequences, because there was no knowing how he'd react. Well, that had been before he'd invaded her space, incensing her desire to a steady burn.

Shit, shit, *shit.*

She wanted him.

Zach's father.

The last time she'd felt the intoxicating pull of desire, she'd given in.

And fallen pregnant with Zach.

The son Ethan didn't know about.

Because she'd decided not to tell him.

'Holy fucking shit,' she muttered, lowering her head between her knees as her throat closed over again.

Ethan had left all those years ago and hadn't come back. And the practical part of her hadn't wanted him to. Not when her belly had swollen, or when her screaming baby boy had torn his way into the world. She'd searched once, but hadn't again in fear of what she'd find. A criminal, an addict, a young man she wouldn't trust within fifty feet of her precious boy.

Her own mother had put her and Regan up for adoption due to drugs. Call her twice shy.

She'd told herself she would hunt him down, one day, just not yet, not before she felt capable of handling the consequences.

The wrong decision. If she'd found him, she would never have believed him dead. That mistake had prevented a man from watching his son grow—prevented Zach from knowing his father.

When Stevie finally emerged from the stall, she found Regan leaning against the basin, arms crossed and gaze fixed on the tiled floor.

'Shit,' Stevie murmured, stopping.

'So you've been saying.' Regan looked up, brown eyes cautious. 'You okay?'

Stevie sniffed, totally busted, and said, 'Yep.'

Regan watched as Stevie moved to the mirror, pressing the thick of her thumbs beneath her eyes. 'Is this about me being back?'

Dismay broke through Stevie's distress as she faced her sister. 'Of course not.'

'Because even Felix thinks it's weird that you want to spend this week on your own. He said you and him were going to hang out, you know, before I came back.'

Only because she hadn't lined the job up yet. 'It's not about you.' But, of course, it seemed that way. Yay for another complication.

'We haven't seen each other since we were teenagers, and you want to be by yourself?' Regan's voice was weak. 'What else could it be about?'

Stevie closed her eyes. 'Something else.'

'Something else, like your sister hooking up with your best friend? Because you were choking on your own sobs in there. Like your heart was being torn into strips.'

Sounded about right.

'Are you in love with Felix?' The question from Regan was a whisper.

'No.' Stevie ran a hand roughly over her face. 'I'm happy about you and him, cross my heart.' She even tried to smile, but Regan's frown told her she hadn't pulled it off.

'You know what else I noticed?' Her sister hadn't un-crossed her arms.

Stevie waited.

'This morning, when I commented on your overloaded bag, you said it was mostly stuffed with beach nibbles. Which, one would assume, you'd have eaten in the eight hours you were out, but it didn't look much different when you got back this afternoon.'

Stevie pressed her lips together. Heavy-duty overalls and work boots weren't great space savers.

'And although you ordered pizza and went through the motions of raising it to your face just now, you didn't eat it. So if you want me to believe that this breakdown isn't about Felix or me,' Regan said, 'then you'll have to tell me where you really were today.'

Stevie groaned. Regan had run away at sixteen and missed Zach's entire childhood. She'd gone off the rails before then, distancing herself and severing the sisterly connection they'd previously shared. She hadn't been a proper part of Stevie's life for the best part of a decade.

But she did have a nightmarish explanation, and she'd braved coming home again. She'd also been polite enough not to ask about Zach's father these past few days, and Stevie hadn't found the right moment to spill without Zach around.

Apparently, now was the time to let her sister be her sister again.

Stevie fisted her hands and explained all, minus the paint job. No need to pull her financial position out for review—her moral and emotional circumstances were more than enough. She rounded off facts like bullet points in an effort to distance herself. It almost worked. How bad could the situation be if she could break it down into ten-word segments?

'That's really, really bad,' Regan finally said, looking dazed.

Yeah. Okay.

At some point during the story, Regan had taken Stevie's hand and squeezed. The touch absorbed some of Stevie's panic, and she breathed a little easier.

'How are you going to tell him?'

Stevie's inhale was shaky. 'Don't suppose I could just not tell him?'

Regan's head tilted, sympathetic.

'Didn't think so,' she muttered.

'And Zach?'

'I should tell Ethan first. The last thing Zach needs is to find out his dad is alive and in town—and doesn't want anything to do with him. I need to know what Ethan wants first.'

'Okay. You need anything, you let me know.' Regan's eyes narrowed as she shook her head. 'I can't believe it. Ethan bloody Rafters. I told him not to touch you. I told him *that night* not to go anywhere near you.'

'I went near him.' Stevie rubbed a hand over her nose. 'And yeah, actually, could you and Felix pick up Zach from the program tomorrow? And explain it all to Felix?'

'Sure.' Her sister squeezed her hand again and let go. As they moved toward the exit, she said, 'Oh, heads-up. Zach almost barged in here before. I grabbed him at the door, but he looked upset.'

'Thanks.' He could throw stones, but he couldn't handle it when they caused damage.

Back at the booth, Felix and Zach looked up together, one seriously concerned, the other seriously stricken. Some kind of communication passed from Regan to Felix, because he slid out of the booth, murmured in Stevie's ear, 'I don't know what's going on, but you need help, you tell me,' and left with Regan's hand in his.

Exhausted, Stevie sat down beside her son. 'Are we okay, Zach?'

He toyed with the cat's ear, avoiding her eye. 'We're good, I guess.' He sounded contrite. 'Why? Are you breaking up with me?'

'No way,' she said. 'I'd never get my Björk shirt back.'

'Good. 'Cause, like you say, we've got to stick together, you and me.'

Panic gripped her again. She focused on inhaling. Exhaling.

'I'm sorry I made you feel bad on purpose,' he mumbled, turning to head-butt her in the arm. His forehead stayed against her. Sighing, she gathered him in close and pressed her lips to his crown.

'That's okay.' She closed her eyes, breathing him in. 'Was your day that bad?'

'No. It was kinda fun. One of the leaders offered to take a pic of me surfing tomorrow so you can see. He's cool.'

'Make sure you say thanks.'

'I thought I'd kick him in the shin. But say thanks, you reckon? Fine.'

'You punk.'

'You crybaby.'

She snorted, and he relaxed, pulling back with a tentative smile.

'Love you,' she said, elbowing him casually in the side.

He gave a cry of outrage, clutched his ribs, and collapsed onto the empty booth beside him. The cat leapt away with a yowl, and Stevie snatched up Zach's foot, tickling, holding firm when he squirmed and squealed. 'No, stop, *stop!*' When she didn't, his begging became melodramatic. 'Okay, please, I'll confess. I'll confess!'

She paused, brow rising.

Slanting a glance up at her, he sighed in exaggerated resignation. 'I love you, too.'

She didn't take that one for granted.

Chapter Three

L ATER THAT NIGHT, Felix sent her a text.

Out in the hall.

Far from sleep, Stevie slid out of bed, crept across the room, and found her best friend waiting in the empty corridor outside. His arms crossed as she faced him, his features stunned. He hadn't even wasted time putting his glasses on. With messed-up hair and T-shirt askew over light sweatpants, he looked like a man roused from bed by an unavoidable disaster.

Fire, burglary, return of the dead—much of a muchness.

'Hey,' she whispered.

'Ethan?' He whispered the name, moving toward her. 'Regan just said—Ethan?'

She rolled her lips between her teeth and knew her helpless silence was answer enough.

'He died.' Felix's skin was pale. 'Years ago.'

She wrapped an arm around her middle. 'His brother.'

Felix's face showed the same horror that had brutalized her that morning. Silent, swallowing her own panic, she ran a consoling hand down his arm.

'But that—' He shook his head, eyes wide. 'He's alive? Here?'

Nodding felt like moving stone, but she managed it.

Felix turned and pressed his forehead against the corridor wall. Eyes pressed shut, features scrunched. 'Holy hell.'

Stevie waited, body heavy.

'How will you—I mean, how do you even—tell him?'

With a throat full of sorrow, she heaved her shoulders up in a shrug.

'Okay,' he said, facing her and taking her hands. 'We've got this, okay? Whatever happens, I'm here for you. I'll always be here for you.' He pulled her into a hug, and she pressed her face into his shoulder.

'I'm counting on it,' she whispered.

ETHAN DIDN'T SLEEP. Disrupted by the thoughts skimming through his head, he couldn't concentrate either. Awake, alert, but unable to focus. Winning combination.

He didn't stay in bed. No point when his head was like this. He paced, he tried to get work done, he picked up his latest handheld brainteaser. They generally helped him focus: something to occupy his excess brain activity while keeping his hands busy. He moved onto the balcony, breathing in the mild night air and seeking comfort in the consistent crash of waves. This puzzle was a metallic cube—complicated, maze patterns for walls, a rod protruding from within—careful manipulation required.

It ended up in the garden bed beneath the balcony.

At three in the morning, he started the electric sander and continued where Stevie had left off. His thoughts kept skimming as he worked.

Stevie—Melbourne—Sydney—selling the house—Hack coping in the new apartment—painting—Stevie—sexy overalls—damn surf program—rising oceanic salt levels—powerlessness—desperation—Stevie—must be different this time—leaving town—too many thoughts—Robin Williams' little spark of crazy—moving, always moving—the almighty ache beneath his ribcage—Stevie—Stevie—Stevie.

He didn't fare well the following day.

Bored by his morning run, he turned back after a few minutes, much to Hack's bewilderment. He burned the toast three times because he kept walking away, and then brushed his teeth for fifteen minutes because he made the mistake of hitting the browser on his phone. His assistant called at precisely eight-thirty, reminding him of critical communications, and by the time he'd handled those calls and emails, Ethan was running very late for helping Vik—curse it, he was always late—so he left the front door unlocked with a note on the doorknob saying Stevie could let herself in and get going.

All he wanted was to talk to her. See her smile, hear that infectious laugh again, and ease the strange sensation that he was missing something.

Instead, he spent the day with an insomniac's hangover,

eyes gritty and skull heavy, helping kids stand on surfboards. He cooked the barbeque for lunch, and while everyone sat around eating and laughing, he stood where grass met sand, staring out at the water and hating the thought that Stevie might be gone when he got home. Every passing minute wound his tension tighter.

'You're jiggling.'

Ethan snapped back to the present. Zach was sitting on the sand in his wetsuit, hair plastered to his forehead, chewing on a burger, another clutched in his other hand.

'I am,' he answered.

'You do it a lot.'

His leg kept moving as he said, 'It's when I stop that's the problem.'

Zach's eyes were narrowed against the glare of the sun. He twisted toward Ethan, raised a hand to shade his eyes, and took another bite. 'What happens?' he asked around the mouthful.

Ethan thought about it. 'You know when you sit still, your eye is caught by the thing that moves the most?'

'Like cars driving past?'

'Yeah. Like fast cars.'

'Fast cars are dangerous.'

'Exactly. It's better if I'm the thing moving.'

Zach frowned. 'Is that why you're moving to Sydney?'

Surprise had Ethan frowning back at him. 'How'd you know that?'

'Heard Vikas talking about your farewell party.'

Ethan glared at the back of his friend's head. He'd said no party. It was easier to move on when he wasn't reminded of what he was leaving behind. 'Overhear any details?'

Zach pulled a face. 'Uh-uh. It's a surprise.'

'Few sentences too late for that, mate.'

He paused mid-chew. 'Oh, man. Don't tell Vikas.'

Ethan smiled.

'You still cool to get a shot of me surfing?'

'Sure.'

Zach dug inside his backpack and passed over a smartphone with a cracked screen.

Ethan took it. 'There's a place in town that could fix this.'

'Mum won't get it fixed. Says I'll just drop it again.' The boy shrugged. 'It's my friend's old one, anyway. He's a programmer, so his work gives him the newest models, and he gives his old ones to Mum and me. It's cool because Mum likes to see where I am on the map, so she's not about to take it away from me. Guaranteed game time.' He gave a fist pump.

Apps designed for parents to stalk their own children. What a world. 'We'll get some good shots.'

The kid said, 'Thank you,' and extended his fist.

Amused, Ethan bumped his knuckles. 'Just don't fall off.'

When he gave the phone back a few hours later, it contained a series of shots that should make Zach's mum proud.

As the group of kids dispersed into the crowded beach, Ethan set to gathering the wetsuits.

'I can help.' Zach tucked a surfboard under each arm, flashing a glance up at Ethan. Then he climbed off toward the clubhouse.

Frowning, Ethan scanned the beach. Poor kid. Couldn't his mum be on time? Distractedly, he met the eyes of a blonde woman strolling along the sand hand in hand with a man. Thinking she looked vaguely familiar, his gaze lingered.

So did hers. She froze midstep, gripping the arm of her companion as Ethan's mind jumped.

Brown eyes—heavy, black eyeliner—challenging chin tilt— genetic resemblance—defiant drunk girl warning him off her sister—Regan—man beside her—glasses and shoes with laces— nerd from school—Stevie's friend—eternal jealousy—Felix.

Ethan shifted backwards.

Regan had changed. No dyed black hair or hard scowl. Easy to miss after this long, and even though Stevie said she'd spent Christmas with her sister, explaining her presence in Byron Bay, his stomach still turned, uneasy.

The pair looked stunned. Had Stevie mentioned him? He caught himself. Of course not. They'd spent one night together—a night she'd likely kept to herself. Admitting to sleeping with a guy like Ethan wouldn't have done her any favors. They were probably struggling to reconcile the Ethan they'd known in high school with the man currently draped in kids' wetsuits.

Weirded out, he raised a hand to acknowledge the pair.

No need to approach. The world didn't have to get that small.

Vik appeared at his shoulder. 'You go meet your painter ex,' he said. 'I'll pack up.'

He didn't need persuading. 'Thanks.'

On his way to the road, he passed Zach coming the other way. They fist-bumped goodbye, grinning.

He clocked a personal best running home. Breathing hard, Ethan crested his balcony to the smell of fresh paint and loud indie music. He hung his sticky shirt over the railing and stepped inside, finding Stevie with feet on separate rungs of the ladder, overalls rolled to mid-calf, and a paint tray in hand. Her shoulders moved in time with the beat, and he could hear her singing, low and mostly on key. Captivated, he imagined claiming the opposite side of the ladder and kissing her over the frame, the lack of bodily contact turning from teasing to torturous in seconds.

Ethan shook the image off as Hack spotted him from the middle of the floor. Stevie jumped at the dog's sudden bark, her expression shuttering as she turned.

'Hey.' He rubbed Hack's ears before moving toward her.

Her attention snapped down to his approaching form and back to his face. 'Hey.'

He halted beside the ladder and placed his hand on the rung beside her boot. 'Didn't have to leave at four today?'

She shook her head. 'Didn't have to wear a shirt today?'

Smiling, he glanced around the half-painted space. 'You

work fast.'

'I've had practice. And the sanding pixie finished for me overnight.' She set the tray on the top of the ladder, twisting to face him, and Ethan found himself at eye level with the cradle of her hips.

Grab her—legs around his waist—hot—against the wall—overalls falling—slick skin—now.

His breathing changed. Lust spilled hot inside him.

'You're standing close,' she commented into the silence.

Ethan didn't move. 'You've always been my kind of beautiful, Stevie.'

She breathed out a wry laugh. 'That's not one of my adjectives.'

'It is to me.'

The cynicism on her face accused him of false flattery. 'You find my laborer's clothes beautiful?' She raised a paintbrush and an ironic brow. 'And my job?'

'Yes,' he said.

She paused. Confusion triggered her brow down.

'I've thought about nothing but you since yesterday morning,' he said, 'and wanted nothing else.'

'Ethan.' His name was a pained breath. 'I told you I can't.'

'Because it won't be different?' His grip tightened on the ladder. It was already different. 'We didn't talk about it last time. We just did it. So we'll talk, figure it out, because this is a second chance, and I don't want to waste it.'

She startled him by jumping down, boots thudding on the hardwood floor. A rush of air moved over him, whisper soft and so gently sweet that it disarmed him of clear thought. Distracted, he watched her run her hands over her hips and bend to roll the hems of her overalls up to her knees. Straightening, she said quietly, 'Then let's talk.'

Progress.

'Forewarning—it's not going bring us together.'

'I'll be the judge of that.'

'Yeah.' Anxiety flickered across her face. 'I know.'

Curious, Ethan led the way to the outdoor wooden table. Face pale, Stevie sat, shifted, and after a sharp exhale, ended up standing with a hand pressed to her face. It was the kind of face push Ethan knew too well, a rough attempt to shove entire truths out of his head. She lowered her hand, cursing.

Not good.

Wary, he asked, 'You okay?'

No jest was in her voice when she said, 'Definitely not.'

Ethan waited, concerned. Her breathing was fast, her skin tacky. 'What's up, Stevie?'

'I...' She faced him. Looked down at the deck. Patted her sides as if she'd forgotten something until her hands balled, pressing against her hips. 'So you know how you asked whether I had a boyfriend or husband or someone?'

He nodded, wariness rising.

'Well, I don't. But there is someone else.' Her voice cracked. 'Someone who makes my life worthwhile. Someone

I love more than I ever thought I could love anyone. He's my world. And I should have told you about him sooner. So much sooner.'

Disappointment pulled at Ethan's shoulders, but he nodded again, because he knew he should. 'He's a lucky man,' he said, meaning it.

'He's not a man yet.' She raised her hands to her stomach, looking ill. 'I have a son, Ethan.'

Ethan was still nodding.

He stopped. 'A son?'

Her head jerked. The hands on her stomach became fists, pressing inward.

A flurry of reaction blew through him, stirring up caution, uncertainty, and then comprehension. Stevie was a single mother. He had both a lifetime of experience with single mothers, and none at all. He'd been raised by one. But he'd never dated one. It explained her reluctance to admit their attraction. Vik used the wellbeing of his children to make decisions, big and small. It seemed Stevie also put her son first, including over her own desires.

'That—that's great, Stevie. Yeah, that's—wow.' He stood, not sure how this kind of thing went. Should he hug her? 'I'm really happy for you.'

She took a step back, gripping the steel railing and closing her eyes.

He stood and reached out, but then let his hand fall. 'You all right?'

'He's yours, Ethan.'

For a solid six seconds, her words were meaningless. He continued to frown at the pallor of her skin, the dark circles beneath her eyes. He wondered how she could grip the sun-heated railing like that without scalding her palms. Her words didn't register, because they made no sense. Then her eyes opened, and her look of utter devastation forced him to rewind to figure out what caused it.

He's yours, Ethan.

The world snapped down to a single point.

Nothing existed but the woman in front of him—and the agony suddenly rallying an army in his chest.

His lips moved. No sound came out.

Stevie swallowed. The tendons in her neck were taut. 'You're the father of my son.'

Ethan forced himself to process those words. He was the father of her son. *No.* That wasn't right. 'It was once,' he said coarsely, and then sat down, as if dismissing the notion. 'We used protection.'

'I thought the pill was effective immediately.' Her voice wavered. 'Stupid. It was my fault.'

'No.' Shaking his head awoke the high-pitched buzz of incomprehension. The agony in his chest grew stronger—an army fit to march into the depths of his soul and shed blood. 'Must have been someone else.'

'There was no one else.'

He shook his head again. His only power over the situation was denial. 'It's not possible.'

'That's what I said.' She was still gripping the railing, and he realized it must be scalding her. That she wanted it to. Her palms would blister. 'But it happened anyway.'

No. No way.

He continued to shake his head, face lowering to stare down at the deck between his knees. *Keep shaking. Just keep shaking, and it'll be okay.*

'Ethan.'

'I can't.'

'He's seven,' she said, voice breaking.

Seven. Like a cut bolt, that threw open the gates to reality. It sucked him in like a vacuum. His mind was pulled apart by the force.

Seven years old—a dad—Stevie hadn't told him—a son—Stevie was a mum—to his son—why hadn't she told him—Beau would never be an uncle—all this time—his head hurt—what should he do—why now—a son—he was a—

'I'm not understanding this.' He heard his own voice, distant.

'I'm sorry.' Stevie's shadow was small on the deck.

He raised his head and met her eyes, dark with culpability. Her fists had returned to her stomach, digging inwards. She'd borne his child and not told him. That was like a heart attack in his head. But instead of his body betraying him, it was Stevie.

'Wait.' He leaned forward, grasping his skull. 'I have a son.'

Her 'yes' was breathless.

His muscles, rarely content to sit still, threw him to his feet. Stevie tilted her chin, clearly prepared to accept whatever onslaught he deemed appropriate. When he said nothing, just stared, she said, 'I'm sorry,' with a helpless shake of her head.

Sorry.

She was sorry.

'That word has no meaning in this situation,' he said.

She didn't deny that.

Desperate to move, he started pacing. 'After three months, six months, sorry was yours. After nine months, yeah, okay, you can be sorry about that. With a newborn in your arms, I would have accepted sorry. First birthday, we'd have been stretching the sincerity of the definition. But eight years. Eight years? Sorry doesn't exist.'

She didn't answer. Didn't move. He suspected she didn't breathe.

The buzzing was growing louder. Before long, this would be beyond him.

'How is it that you—what could possibly—who doesn't tell a guy he got her pregnant?' His voice rose, lifted by the arms of insult. 'Who *does* that to someone?'

'It wasn't about you.' Tears stood in her eyes, but they didn't fall. 'It was about my baby. What was best for him.'

He froze amidst his shattered rage and very quietly said, 'Explain that.'

'I looked you up when I first found out,' she said, fraught. 'Ethan Rafters, right there on Facebook. Profile picture of a whiskey bottle between a woman's breasts. Posts about getting wasted and raving until sunrise, posts made after you'd moved away. You weren't getting your life on track, Ethan; you were throwing it away. I wasn't going to contact a guy like that.'

It dawned on him that he wasn't breathing right. Too shallow, trying to match the speed of his pulse, his thoughts. He wanted to run, fast across the beach, separating himself from the teenager he had been. His fingers curled into fists as he fought to focus.

'I closed that account.' After a furious visit from Beau, an argument he'd never forget, and a brainstorming session that had birthed his first business. Clearly, it hadn't happened soon enough. 'I changed.'

Then a different shred caught his attention. 'Wait. What do you mean, *a guy like that?*'

She didn't answer, lips pinched.

'How much could I have changed in the weeks since you'd slept with me?'

She looked appalled.

It slammed him. 'You thought I was a scumbag the whole time.'

She shook her head, tears falling.

'You did. You must have. Or else you'd have contacted me anyway.'

She ducked her head.

He felt like she'd gouged out his pride with a pitchfork. Appropriate weapon for the monster she'd thought he was. 'I can't believe this.'

'I've regretted it every second since—' She stopped herself.

'Since I *died*?' Incredulity took on a scathing tone.

His thoughts were starting to scatter. He was too worked up—couldn't think straight.

'I was going to contact you,' she said, speaking fast. 'I was, I swear. But it was so hard. Regan had run away, and my foster parents didn't care, so I was living with Felix. I didn't figure out I was pregnant until I was five months, so the doctors recommended against—' She stopped. 'I dropped out of uni when I found out. I was so scared. We had no money. No one to help. My whole life bottomed out from under me. I only had energy for things that could help me, and I didn't think you could. You'd told me yourself that you weren't good for me.'

The pitchfork pierced into his memory of their night together and stirred. It turned muddy with this knowledge of how Stevie had really viewed him.

Incapable. A screw up. Unworthy of her child.

Of his own child.

The agony army reached its target. It fought dirty, and something collapsed beneath his solar plexus. His heart. His pride. The remaining dregs of self-respect for his past self;

the foundations of his life as he knew it. He pressed a hand over the carnage.

He shut his eyes for a moment, closed his mind, tried to block it out. But he'd never had that kind of control. He'd been a teenage train wreck, careening out of control on the rails of recklessness. All these years, he thought he'd avoided the crash.

And here, now, the impact of lost fatherhood.

'I have to swim,' he gasped, and he moved around her.

He was halfway down the balcony steps when she called out behind him. 'Now?'

Now more than ever.

'Ethan.' Her boots pounded on the wooden steps behind him. 'You're running away from this?'

He staggered along the sandy track leading to the shore, calling out over his shoulder, 'I can't think standing still.'

Her footfalls gained on him, and then she was at his shoulder, keeping up, saying, 'My foster care didn't involve love. I knew what it was like to have parents who didn't give a damn about me. My son wasn't going to have that from his dad. You were messed up, Ethan. You know you were.'

Oh, he knew.

He reached the sand at full speed, struck by the heat of the afternoon sun. He headed straight for the waves.

Stevie slowed as he reached the water. 'What support could you have given us?'

Loathing the answer to that question, he ploughed

straight into the sea. The liquid embraced him as he dove, the summer water too mild to shock his skin. He kicked, pushing himself deeper until his hands touched sand, and the pressure in his head was rivaled by the need to surrender to buoyancy.

Finally, he gave up. He surfaced.

'Ethan.'

Drenched, he turned toward the shore. Stevie was wading in, boots discarded on the beach. The waves were quick to coat her hips, her overalls, and then it was just her head above water, her blonde hair flaring brightly as she reached him, treading water.

'You can't run away from this.' Water lapped over her shoulders.

'Not running.' He treaded water, legs working to hold steady in the waves. 'Coping.' Then he asked, 'What's his name?' Everything within him paused to hear it.

Her head tipped back as her movements slowed, body sinking momentarily. She didn't answer.

'You won't tell me his name?' That hurt, everywhere.

'If you know his name, you'll build an idea of him around it. You'll start thinking you know him. You'll start thinking—'

'That he's my son?' he cut her off loudly.

Her features broke, but no tears joined the seawater on her face. 'You'll imagine what he's like. What you'll say to him when you meet him. What he'll say to you. But it won't go like that. However you imagine it, it's not what would happen.'

He deliberately reused her tense of a hypothetical. 'What *would* happen?'

'He's protective of me. He won't deal easily.'

'So, you didn't tell him about me? After yesterday?'

Her dark eyes were heavy with apology.

'So he—he still thinks I'm dead?'

She slipped under the surface a little as she nodded.

Ethan's insides churned, and he increased the speed of his legs. A protective son who believed him dead. 'He'll hate me.'

She looked pained. 'He's seven. His world is a cocoon made up of his mother, school, and video games. He'll be confused. It'll be sudden—but he'll try to figure out what it means for him. For his routine. For our lives. And when he's confused, he gets upset and tries to reject the thing confusing him.'

Which would be Ethan.

'Has he ever asked about me?' The words hurt his throat.

'He did.' Her squinted gaze shifted over his face, an attempt to predict his reaction. 'And I told him that his dad and I were young. That neither of us planned to have a family so soon, or to be each other's family. I—' Water lapped over her chin, her mouth. 'I told him you were smart and a good guy, but that you made bad choices.'

He swallowed, tasting bitterness and brine. 'And those

choices got me killed.'

'It's what I've always believed, Ethan.'

His brain hit a wall. Swimming wasn't going to clear his head. 'Will you tell him?'

'If you want me to,' she said, after a moment's hesitation.

Defensive anger filled him. 'Why wouldn't I want you to?'

'God, I don't know!' She raised her chin. Red rimmed her eyes and white paint speckled her nose. 'I don't know anything right now. This shouldn't even be possible, but, suddenly, you're alive and here, and I still want you, and I don't understand what that means, or if it means anything at all. I did the wrong thing back then, because I thought I knew you, but I didn't—why the hell would you want me to predict what you'd want now?'

He had no idea.

He was stuck on *and I still want you.*

She continued treading water, voice shaking. 'I couldn't predict how you'd react, okay? What if you weren't interested? Too little, too late? You're moving—got some exciting project lined up. I'm not about to tell him about his dad, only to follow up with the fact you're moving on in a week or two, and you don't want to see him. I can't mess him up like that. It has to be about him, before either of us, Ethan. Always him first.'

That got through the mess in his head.

He stopped treading, went under, and breathed out. He

sank.

'I'll tell him.' She spoke when he resurfaced, her voice softer now, defeated. 'But I need to know what you want. Do you just want to meet him, or do you want more than that? Because the former isn't an option. I swear to tell him, if you want more.'

All or nothing.

Ethan ran a hand over his eyes and ended up face pushing, desperate to shove these thoughts out of his head. They were loud, shrill, forbidding him to ever know quiet again. But silence was the only way he'd be able to figure out how he felt—what he wanted Stevie to do.

He needed time and a clear head. Two things he lacked.

'I'm not coping,' he muttered, turning his back and staring blindly at the horizon. 'I need space.'

He heard her shaky inhale. The soft lap of water on her floating body. Then a light splash as she twisted, taking off toward the shore.

'Stevie,' he said, not turning.

The splashing paused.

'Don't come to work tomorrow. I need to think.'

Chapter Four

VIK OPENED THE door on the second knock. He wore loose yoga pants, no shirt, and an eight-month-old on his hip. Despite the hollering in the background, he looked unfazed at his friend's after-dinner arrival.

'Hey,' he greeted, bouncing slightly.

Muscle memory enabled Ethan to say, 'Hey.'

'You okay?'

No. He was all wrong. 'I'm breaking.'

'From a run?'

Fair assumption. His chest heaved and his sweat-drenched singlet was plastered to his chest. Fatigue tremors had long set in, an unheeded physical warning. 'That's not what I meant.'

Running hadn't helped.

He was still breaking.

Vik frowned, and his eyes seemed to adjust to the dim porch light. That was when the baby was passed to his wife, a few strict instructions delivered to his other two kids, and then he ushered Ethan into his meditation garden, forcing him down onto a finely embroidered cushion. Mosaic features edged the paving stones around them, carefully crafted designs of teal, tan, and plum. A fountain trickled serenely near the vine-coated garden wall, and Ethan breathed in, trying to find peace in the zest of mint and cardamom leaves in the air.

Peace wasn't forthcoming. He'd still be running if his body would take it.

His friend sat cross-legged beside him, skin dark in the moonlight. 'What's happened?'

Ethan's voice was hollow. 'Teach me how to time travel.'

Vikas didn't answer. His silence was tense.

'I need to go back eight years.'

A pause. Then, 'Is this about the painter?'

He made a strained sound. It meant yes.

'You wish you hadn't slept with her?'

'No.' Despair drowned him. 'I wish I'd stayed with her.'

Vik gave a soft, 'Oh.'

In the past few hours, Ethan had been accosted by images. Moments that would never happen. A small hand seeking his. Playing with a sprinkler on the lawn in summer, Stevie laughing, half-soaked in one of Ethan's old shirts. Putting their son to sleep, and then sneaking into bed, languorous and as quiet as they could manage.

Foolish thoughts, because in no reality would they have happened.

If Stevie had contacted him at eighteen, bearing news of a baby, he'd have freaked out. Run a mile, and then run a thousand more. He hadn't been ready to settle down. He'd barely been able to sit down.

He'd left home with fresh underwear, an intangible dream, and shit-all life skills. And if he hadn't run from Stevie, he'd have made her situation worse. He might have tried. God, he hoped he'd have tried. But he'd have been in no position to support her or a child.

She'd known it. So she'd chosen to be a single mother. No sharing the workload and worries of parenthood—no snatches of rest when she was off duty. Always cooking and cleaning, always teaching and entertaining. Always working. Ethan's mum had slaved away for the best part of her young years, keeping him and Beau fed and schooled. He couldn't imagine how hard a life it must be.

And it had been Stevie's better option.

That truth hung from him like a lead weight in the ocean.

'She had my baby,' he whispered.

Vik made a strange sound, that wasn't so strange considering.

In the stunned silence that followed, Ethan's face tightened, his throat burned, and tears came hot to his eyes. He gave himself over to several gut-deep sobs before swallowing the pain down and pressing the thick of his thumb to his forehead, his breathing far from steady.

'He's seven,' he said.

Vik gripped his shoulder, squeezed, and withdrew.

'Where is he?'

Ethan gaped at him. 'I didn't ask.'

Too preoccupied by the brain-crushing concept of having a son in general, he hadn't thought about the reality of having a son right now.

Stevie had said she was visiting friends. So that could mean he'd stayed behind at a friend's house. Or that he was here, in Byron Bay.

Here…in Byron Bay.

Ethan was going to be sick.

'Okay,' his friend said quickly, because Ethan had gone fetal. 'Here's what we'll do. Ten minutes of breathing, so you don't pass out. Twenty minutes of talking, so you don't implode. Then, we'll go for a drive to take your mind off it.'

Ethan groaned.

They both knew his mind didn't work like that.

STEVIE TOOK ZACH for a long walk. Three and a half hours long. She needed to be out in the open, moving. Emotions struck hardest in an idle body, and she didn't want the unknown to consume her. Besides, she could distract Zach with physical activity. Sitting still, he'd pick her anxiety up in minutes.

They reached the lighthouse in a series of running races. Waited for the sun to sink, and then watched darkness swallow the sky. They kicked off their flip-flops and waded into the water, playing join the dots with the stars and dropping to their knees, reveling in the waves that crashed cool over their chests. Zach was so happy he turned silly, pretending to be a shark and attacking her with arms latched tight around her waist. He bit at her stomach with lip-covered teeth, and she feigned distress even as she kept a hold on him.

After a while, he relaxed, floating on his back and using her as an anchor.

It should have been bliss. Instead, hollowed out by the emotional blade of that afternoon, Stevie felt numb. She stared at the moon and saw Ethan's ashen face; watched over and over the devastating twist of his features that had carried him from dazed to anguished at the news of a son.

It was after ten when she led the way back to the hotel. Zach walked several paces behind her, stepping in her sandy footprints. 'Want to skip the program tomorrow?' she asked over her shoulder.

'What?' He aborted the game to leap up beside her. 'Seriously?'

'Seriously.' She peeled her wet singlet off her skin. When she let go, it stuck again. 'We can do whatever you want.'

He fist pumped and struck a power stance. 'Awesome! I'll teach you to surf.'

She made herself smile, walking backwards so she faced him. 'You're a pro now, huh?'

'Total pro. I should charge by the hour. You saw the

pics.'

She had. Zach balancing on the board, arms out to the sides, riding in on a wave. His face one huge grin. 'Surfing it is.'

'That'll be twenty bucks.'

'No problem,' she said. 'Guess now that you're a working man, I'd better start charging you rent.'

He fell to his knees, hands raised like claws to the sky. 'Stella!'

Smiling for real this time, and figuring the exclamation had gone through his school, she said, 'I'll give you twenty right now if you tell me what that's from.'

He sighed, guessed, 'Star Wars?' and proceeded to bounce ahead the rest of the way back, occasionally spinning around with another suggestion for the following day. 'Frisbee on the beach!' and 'Iced chocolate for lunch!'

They entered Lullabar and veered passed the bar toward the staircase that led to the upstairs rooms. Zach then proposed tandem hang-gliding, and Stevie was busy laying down the law regarding exactly how far above the earth's surface her seven-year-old was allowed without a motor when Zach stopped suddenly, foot on the bottom step. Narrowly avoiding a collision, Stevie saw that he was staring back at the bar. Probably considering one last lemonade before bed.

She said, 'No, Zach.'

At the same time he exclaimed, 'Ethan!'

Her heart spasmed.

Dread iced her right through.

No.

Just no.

She turned and met a tormented, tawny gaze. Ethan Rafters sagged on a bar stool, forearms resting on the countertop, one hand clutching a glass of amber liquid. Life-altering news hung off him like hard liquor, adding a glassy sheen to his eyes and weight to his shoulders. His features twinged as his eyes fell to Zach—emotional cramps of shock, disbelief, and sorrow.

Beside him was a stunning Indian man, his wide eyes comprehending the relevance of the unfolding situation. He placed a hand over Ethan's shoulder, possibly as reassurance, possibly to keep him upright. Probably both.

'And Vikas!' Zach twisted to look up at Stevie, hand tugging at hers. 'Mum. Ethan and Vikas are instructors at the program. Come meet them.'

Instructors at the program.

Ethan and Zach had already met.

On dead feet, she was led four interminable steps to the bar.

'Hey guys,' Zach said amiably, resting a hand against the empty stool on the end.

Ethan looked down at him, somehow managing to nod in wordless greeting. He looked well and truly wasted. Stevie's gut wrenched.

'This is my mum. She said I could have tomorrow off, so I won't see you 'til Thursday.'

Vikas darted a glance at Ethan, who was staring at Zach through hopeless eyes, and said calmly, 'That's fine, Zach. We'll be onto learning circus acts by then.' He looked to Stevie, dark gaze measuring. 'It's nice to meet you.'

She rested a hand on the counter, letting it take some of the weight pressing down on her. 'Thanks for teaching Zach.'

The conversation was meaningless. The real action was happening in Ethan's head as he saw and recognized his son for the first time. He'd half-turned toward him, one forearm still spread out on the bar.

'Ethan,' Zach said, frowning a little. 'You'll be there Thursday, right?'

Ethan stared as if Zach had just asked for his dying breath.

Zach's frown turned uneasy. 'You okay?'

'I didn't know,' Ethan finally answered, words broken.

Stevie curled a hand around her son's shoulder. 'Neither does he.'

At that, Ethan's gaze made its way up, burdening her with enough blame to bury her.

'What?' Zach could feel when subtext grazed the top of his head. His eyes narrowed between them. 'Mum?'

Vikas spoke. 'Ethan was just helping out with the surfing component. We were one instructor down. He's finished helping now.'

'Oh.' Zach looked down, running his toes through an unidentifiable liquid on the bar floor.

Stevie squeezed his shoulder. A crowded room was not the place to introduce him to his father. 'Do you mind if I chat with these guys, Zach?'

After another wary glance at Ethan, he shrugged, said, 'Shotgun the shower,' and darted upstairs.

The venue bustled around them, half-full with people eating together, drinking together. It wasn't the sit-alone-and-wallow kind of bar. It was a beachside hot spot, attracting tourists and locals with urban-grime décor, laid-back vibes, and house-made pizzas.

Ethan stood out as the pathetic drunk crumpled on the counter.

Vikas's eyes travelled between the pair. 'I'm just gonna…' And he wandered off to one of the booths with his beer.

Stevie stood, dismayed, wordless. There was no precedent for this. When Ethan finally spoke, she expected blame, accusations for not telling him about Zach all those years ago, harsh and hurt words to unburden his troubled soul. Instead, he blinked those long lashes at her and said, 'I'm so sorry, Stevie.'

She frowned as nearby laughter drowned out his words. 'What?'

'I'm sorry I caused this.' A few fingers gestured toward

where Zach had stood.

'This?' she repeated with an edge.

'I don't mean Zach.' His cringe was delayed, sodden. 'I mean for the last eight years of your life. I'm sorry I couldn't be there. Supporting you. Helping, somehow.'

Her breath faltered. After everything, *he* felt bad? 'It was my fault for not telling—'

'No,' he interrupted. 'You were right. I couldn't have supported you.' The truth sounded gritty in his throat. 'I would have pulled you down, messed up his childhood. You knew me, Stevie. You knew what you had to do.'

Stunned, her fingers curled around the countertop as more laughter came from down the bar. The sound felt inappropriate, intrusive. Stevie shifted closer as she breathed, 'What?'

'I would've made things worse.' Ethan drank from his glass. 'I'm sorry I was that kind of guy.'

Had the bar stool beside him not been so tall, she would have collapsed onto it. Instead, she clambered up numbly, her wet shorts sticking to the wood as she twisted in toward him. This close to his side, the general chatter formed an aural cocoon, and from within it, she asked quietly, 'Shouldn't you resent me?'

'I resent myself.' He looked at her, eyes the shade of his whiskey and large with its influence. 'I can't imagine how impossible it must've been. That decision. I hate it, but you chose right.'

She swayed as culpability's invisible hold tried to release her, but disbelieving, she held it down.

She'd dealt this man an emotional crisis. Only hours ago, she'd upheaved his life, slammed his self-respect, and left him to deal with it.

And he *was* dealing with it. Admittedly with a loaded dose of alcohol, but he'd braved the chaos in his head to confront the heart of the matter—and there, he'd accepted past faults and harbored no grudge.

Respect roused a physical ache within her, a needy tug, a hot tightening. He had a good soul. And she craved it now, as she'd always craved his body.

'You've done so much,' he said, his forearms sliding across the counter as he plunged into her space. Her pulse tripped as his thigh met hers. His face sagged close, one hand cupping his cheekbone to counter his liquor-loose posture. 'I'm trying to get my head around it. Around you. You had your life mapped out—university, engineering, a career. Instead, I knocked you up and skipped town, and you stepped up and raised an amazing kid.' A strange expression ran down his features. 'Zach. You raised Zach. He's your kid.' His eyes squeezed closed, and Stevie recognized it as heartache.

'He's yours, too,' she murmured.

Pained, he met her gaze. 'I was thinking about it, just before.' Struggle pulled his mouth down into a deep frown. 'You told me to figure out whether I'd want to start something with him. With—Zach. But I'm not cut out for this. I don't think I can.'

Stevie flinched, realizing in that instant that she hadn't expected him to walk away from this.

'It's not that I don't want to.' The sadness in his gaze proved that. 'But I'm no better for him than I was back then.'

She let out a breath. 'Of course you're better. You're doing something with your life, Ethan. You've achieved so much. You own property, a business. You help out in the community.' Her own shortfalls stung her, but she brushed them off. 'You set a good example.'

His head shook, a helpless movement.

Frowning, she waved over the bartender, a man with a swell of black, curly hair, glasses, and a Lullabar-branded shirt. Glancing at his name badge, she said, 'Water, please, Josh?'

He flicked an assessing glance at Ethan and returned with a full jug. Thanking him, Stevie poured a glass and manipulated it into Ethan's hand.

'You've got a lot to deal with.' This news would mess up anyone.

'That's not it.'

'Then what is it?'

'I left home because my head was a mess.' He drained the water, set the glass down. 'And it still is.'

'You left home because you knew you could be better.

And you are.'

'I'm not.'

'Okay.' She moved to refill his glass. 'I'm tired of this drunken self-pity. You need—'

'I have ADHD.'

Her grip on the jug loosened, and it tipped sharply, splashing over the counter. Ethan had attention deficit hyperactive disorder? That—

Made a lot of sense.

Setting the jug down, she eyed him and thought back. Retrospectively, the truth was there. Ethan had always been distracted in class, restless. He'd back-chatted, hadn't done homework, and got detention. Bad home life, everyone assumed—the result of a mother who had no time or inclination to parent. In high school, he'd wagged classes, received suspensions, and drank himself horizontal.

Unless, perhaps, the truth of it was that he hadn't been able to focus. Had fallen behind in class and been told he wasn't smart enough. Easier to become what people expected than to fail at challenging their perceptions.

'I can see it on your face,' he said, watching her.

She frowned. 'What?'

'You think only kids have it.'

'I do not.'

Okay, she kind of did.

'You don't know how disruptive it is,' he said, lowering his face onto his folded forearms. 'It's why I should leave

Zach alone.'

She faced his folded form, setting her elbow on the counter. His chestnut hair was scruffy, tattered by sea salt, and the nape of his neck was summer gold. Desire lurched low in her belly, and she ached to run her fingernails over his scalp, slipping down beneath the collar of his shirt and across the broad sweep of his back.

Balling her hands, she said, 'Tell me about this disruption.'

He looked up, pressing his hand against his forehead. 'I'm off-the-charts crazy. I have all this energy. Can't concentrate. Can't stay in one place. I get bored. I'm incapable of things everyone else finds simple,' he continued as he topped up his water. The countertop received a generous portion. 'I run late; I forget to do the washing; Hack has to ask to be fed. But I don't think twice about flying to California on a whim or singlehandedly renovating an entire house.' He drank. 'Someone like me can't have a kid.'

But he did.

He had Zach.

'Do you want to get to know Zach?' she asked quietly.

It looked like too many possible answers rushed to Ethan's mouth. He shook his head slightly, overwhelmed. 'That's not relevant.'

'It is to me.'

His pause swelled with anguish. 'Of course I do,' he whispered.

Then she'd find a way. It didn't have to be a traditional father-son setup. On the plus side... 'It sounds like you and Zach have been getting along.'

His eyes focused on her, sharp. 'No. Don't.'

'You said you wanted it.'

'I'm not cut out for it.' Ethan had found a decisive tone. 'For him.'

'The thing is, Ethan.' She leaned in, arm brushing his. Sensation flared across her skin. 'I don't believe that.'

'I failed high school.' Spoken like a winning argument.

Stevie nodded, and said, 'You know what I've noticed about our education system? Grades are more a reflection of your organizational skills and ability to concentrate than of your intelligence.'

He stared at her. It was quite a while before he said, 'I never make the bed.'

'Made beds take longer to get into.'

'I can't follow a recipe to save my life. I make it all up.'

'Zach's not fussy. He also enjoys emergency takeaway.'

'I forget things. Important things.'

'I guess they're not really important, then.'

'Trust me, they are. I'm a nutcase,' he told her with the sincerity of a lifetime's belief. 'I can't be a dad.'

Her eyes softened. 'Ethan,' she said, touching his hand briefly. 'I think you've jumped ahead.'

His glance was stricken.

'You know we're not talking about raising a child? You're

not going to be picking him up from school, or soccer practice, or helping him with his homework. You're more likely going to be calling him up every so often or visiting him on weekends.' She watched that truth pull him back. 'There's no huge responsibility. It's just bonding. Which you've done with him so far, without even knowing it.'

Brow etched in consternation, he took a few moments to pour more water and drink it. He found a beer-sodden coaster from further down the bar and placed it down carefully, water glass on top.

Finally, he looked at her. 'I jumped ahead.'

She nodded.

'I'd made a decision. A hard one, but I thought... Now I don't know what any of this means. Again.'

Neither did she, but enlightenment wasn't going to strike tonight. First, he'd drunk too much; second, this problem lacked a shiny solution. 'I think we should get you home.' Stevie peered around Ethan and met Vikas's watchful eye. The man gave a nod and slid out of the booth.

'What if it doesn't mean anything?'

Stevie slid to her feet and eased him off the stool. 'It'll mean something if you want it to. Vikas is going to take you home.'

'What if he doesn't want anything to do with me? What if the closest I get to fatherhood is sending money in an empty birthday card 'cause I won't even know what to write?'

Her heart twisted. 'It won't be like that.'

She had no idea what it *would* be like. But she knew that if this man wanted to be in Zach's life, she'd do her best to make it happen, and she'd deal with the personal consequences later.

He didn't answer, his thoughts folded inward as she brought him to his feet. It was only when she stood, grasping his arms to keep him upright, that she noticed his gaze was strapped to where her damp singlet stuck to her chest, molded to the fabric of her bra. She stilled as awareness pooled between them, muggy, sticky. He was wasted, wallowing in dark thoughts, but the look in his eyes betrayed that even in this state, he'd make her burn.

After all these years, he could still upend her world with a steady glance, shaking loose trivial details like where she was, who she was, and all the reasons surrendering to him would be a bad idea.

All that ever remained was need.

The room faded to grey as Ethan's biceps shifted under her palms. A moment later, his hands reached her waist. His palms spanned her ribcage, her damp singlet a barrier between skin, and he used his wide hold to draw her nearer as he dipped his face too close to hers.

'And then there's this,' he murmured, voice low.

Her body tightened. 'Because things aren't complicated enough.'

'Feels like the only simple thing.'

'It wouldn't afterwards.' Fighting the desire thrumming

through her, she looked away to find Vikas navigating around a group of inebriates.

'I can't stop thinking about you,' Ethan said as she faced him again. Heat crowded their space, tightening with a static charge, and she struggled to fight the pull of his skin, the lure of his mouth. 'I can't lie.' His words were gravelly. 'I want you even more now knowing you've borne my son and raised him.'

Lord, help her.

'So much more,' he said, 'and that shouldn't be possible.'

He leaned in.

Stevie averted her face. In that moment, she hated that her head ruled her body. Seriously, viciously hated it.

'Stevie,' he groaned against her cheek.

'You're drunk.' And they couldn't, not with all their baggage and Zach perched innocently on top.

Vikas appeared at his side, bless him, and Stevie stepped back completely, longing tearing her skin. May her desire bleed out and leave her capable of handling this.

'Hope you sleep well,' she murmured.

His cynical look fell into a nervous frown. 'You said you'd only tell him if I knew what I wanted. And I know I'm not right for him, but...I can do bonding. Maybe, I don't know, maybe I want you to do it anyway.'

Stevie nodded, and was broken by all the ways her life was about to change.

'Tell Zach about me.'

Chapter Five

UPSTAIRS, THE CLOSED bathroom door muted the sound of light splashes. In a daze, Stevie picked up Zach's clothes from the floor and hung them over the balcony to dry in the warm night air. She used a hotel towel to dry the puddle on the floorboards, and then added her own damp clothes to the railing once she'd changed into fresh shorts and a shirt. When she heard the shower start running, she figured Zach must be sitting on the drain so the water would fill to the lip of the shower base. No baths allowed without her nearby, so he'd done the next best thing.

'Zach.' She knocked on the door. 'Will you be long?'

There was a pause. 'You'll probably have to leave my breakfast at the door in the morning.'

'Oh, sure,' she said, 'because in addition to being your cleaner, cook, taxi, bread-winner, and disciplinarian, I also provide room service.'

The water stopped. She heard gentle splashes. 'You sound busy. Feel free to drop the discipline thing.'

She rolled her eyes.

With a grin in his voice, he said, 'Ten more minutes?'

'Okay, but then straight to bed. I'm going to go say goodnight to Felix and Regan.'

'I already did!'

'I said *I'm* going to,' she called.

'Oh, okay.' Then, 'Mum! Is Ethan okay?'

She stiffened. Pressed her palm against the door. Closed her eyes at another innocent splash of water. 'I'm not sure. Maybe we can talk about it in the morning.'

Because before she dropped that bombshell on her son, she needed to process the events of today. In lieu of hard liquor, that meant talking.

'I might be a while,' she added.

'BREATHING EXERCISES AREN'T going to fix this, you know.'

Vik's words were blurry in Ethan's ears. He slumped against the passenger door with his eyes closed, but the vibration of the car was making his skull nauseous. Groaning, he sat up.

'There are poses I could teach you, designed to transmute sexual energy,' his friend spoke again, 'and enhance spiritual cultivation.'

Ethan grunted.

'They won't work.'

His head was starting to pound. He needed more water. His heart was still pounding. He needed Stevie.

'I've never seen you like that with a woman.' As Vik's

words sank in, Ethan turned his head toward him, vague, questioning. 'Your energy changed. You focused on her like she was the only thing in the universe. I know the drinks have you fired up, but there was more between you than that. No amount of spiritual awareness or meditation will ease that, for one very apparent reason.'

Ethan grunted again.

Vik pulled into Ethan's driveway, shut off the engine, and faced him to deliver what had to be Ethan's final piece of life-altering news for the day.

'She's your One.'

ZACH SHIFTED. THE water from his hair dripped around his ear and suctioned him to the door. Mum would be furious if she found him, but Fred and George Weasley had eavesdropped all the time, so he didn't particularly care. It was annoying though, because their voices kept going in and out of focus, so he couldn't figure out what they were talking about. Coming in late hadn't helped.

He knew it was serious. Obviously. His mum didn't cry about nothing, and last night when Regan had blocked him from following her into the bathroom, he'd heard crying going on inside. He hated it—it made him feel unsafe.

Mums weren't supposed to cry.

So far, he'd heard things like *shell-shocked,* and *life changing,* and *going to take time.* He also heard Ethan's name a lot, and his own.

It was totally confusing.

'...*doesn't think he's right for this,*' his mum was saying. '*He's got ADHD...*'

Zach pulled a face. No, he didn't. Colin at school had it, but Zach didn't act anything like that. Colin was funny, and super good in IT class, but he was also a nut bucket.

Frowning, Zach pressed his ear harder against the door.

Felix was speaking. '...*open-minded and see what happens. There's nothing else you can do.*'

Regan said something next, too quiet to hear.

Mum then said something about *not coping* and *about to get worse.*

'What the heck?' Zach muttered to himself, switching to use his other ear.

Felix's voice wafted through, finishing with '...*as bad as you think. He's a good kid.*'

'*But still a kid.*' His mum's voice got louder, closer to the door. '*I'm not coping with this. How can I expect Zach to deal with it? I can't even go on a date without him cracking it. Everyone new is a threat. Now his dad's alive—and here. He's going to hate this.*'

Zach jerked back.

What?

He stared openmouthed at the door, heart pounding, face burning.

His dad was alive? Here? Dating his *mum?*

WHAT?

The ground split beneath him. Tears rushed to his eyes, and he locked his jaw. He took several unsteady breaths before returning to the door.

'...*from the program,*' his mum was saying. '*Zach introduced us, for God's sake. Imagine if he'd known he was introducing his parents.*'

He pulled back again. This didn't make—it made no sense. And what? He hadn't introduced anyone. They just went for a walk; they didn't even—

Zach froze, gut lurching.

Ethan was his *dad?*

ZACH WAS MISSING.

He never went anywhere without telling her. He was a good kid. Because of that, Stevie hadn't thought twice about the light being off when she'd padded back into their room. Oblivious, she'd wasted precious time showering and brushing her teeth, trying not to wake him. She'd been mid-creep out of the bathroom, fingers brushing the light switch, when the spill of light through the half-open door had exposed Zach's empty bed.

Now, with panic beating high in her throat, she fled downstairs, Felix on her tail. The bar was mostly deserted, just a few stragglers finishing last drinks while the staff put away glasses and wiped down the counter. He wasn't here. She knew right away, but she still darted around, looking in all the booths and bathrooms and coming up empty.

'Zach!' Her shout bounced off the high ceiling, more helpless cry than call.

'The guy behind the bar said he left about twenty minutes ago,' Felix spoke from behind her. 'Zach told him he was meeting you outside.' Concern weighted his voice, and Stevie spun, seeing her fear mirrored in his eyes—fear that Zach had overheard and taken off. It was dark out there. What if he went in the water?

Stevie almost collided with Regan as she bolted toward the exit.

'I couldn't find his phone.' Regan rushed out alongside her. 'I tried calling, but he didn't pick up. Here's yours.' She shoved Stevie's phone into her hand.

'Use the map.' Felix's command cut through her scattered panic.

With shaking hands, Stevie opened the tracking app she shared with Zach and clicked on his profile. It refreshed the map, loaded, and zoomed in on his current location.

'Oh, Jesus.'

ETHAN LAY ON his back, the wooden floor hard against his spine and throbbing skull. Hack sprawled beside him, snoring lightly. Plastic drop sheets crackled too loudly in his ears when he shifted, but getting to his bed on the mezzanine was beyond him. He couldn't sleep anyway. He'd had too much water, at the bar, and again at Vik's insistence once they'd arrived home. It had cleared the fog from his mind, leaving him exhausted, hollowed out, and unable to escape the epic revelations of the day.

Zach was his son.

Stevie was his One.

'Bloody hell,' he muttered, because she just might be.

Ethan wasn't long-term relationship material. He knew the statistics. Adults with ADHD were three times more likely to get divorced—on top of the already-high divorce rate. He was more likely to have a drug or alcohol problem—been there, done that. He'd even read that there was a correlation between crime offenders and ADHD.

Basically, he was way more likely to have his life go arse up than someone who was neurotypical.

Ethan hadn't let the stats stop him over the years. He'd met some great women, who tended to find his idiosyncrasies endearing—until they didn't. His insomnia, his forgetfulness, his lack of anything resembling balance threw them off. His hyperfocus had broken his last girlfriend—missing their flight for a weekend getaway because he'd had an 'idea' hadn't gone down well. Since moving to Byron Bay, he'd kept himself a single man.

Because he understood. He really did. At no point did he wonder why his relationships didn't last. No shred of frustration, irritation, or hurt that his exes had thrown at him had come close to what he threw at himself.

He'd tried medication—and had maxed out on the anxiety side effect. Honest-to-God anxiety that had him clenching his jaw so tightly he'd ended up with headaches and joint pain until he hadn't been able to bear it anymore.

He didn't know why the hell he was like this, but he couldn't change it. He closed his eyes, resentment like a pile of hot bullets in his gut. It was the way he was.

And Stevie didn't need it.

A bang from the front of the house had Hack scrabbling confusedly to his feet. The dog stood, lost in between sleep and wakefulness, presumably trying to figure out where the noise had come from. The bang sounded again.

'It's a possum,' Ethan told him, splaying an arm out to the side.

Hack ran off anyway.

Then the doorbell rang, and his dog started barking.

No one would expect a man who'd lived this day to get up and answer the door at such a late hour. Except whoever was at the door. The bell rang again, and again, until he achieved an upright position, staggered down the hall, and hurled it open.

Zach glared up at him. Face puffy, eyes red. Sweat shone on his skin, and his breaths came hard. He held his phone by his side, screen lit up. He looked exhausted, overwhelmed. Frightened.

She'd told him.

'You stay away from my mum.'

Ethan gripped the door, glancing toward the street for a car, expecting to see Stevie watching on anxiously from the driver's seat.

No car. No Stevie.

'How did you…?' He trailed off as Hack muscled his way outside, tail flying.

Zach's eyes darted down. When his attention shot back up, that familiar golden gaze flung him into the center of Ethan's mental hurricane.

This was his son. A boy conceived from his own flesh and blood.

'You made her cry,' Zach accused.

And Stevie's too—he could see Stevie all over him.

'She said you're my dad, but my dad's dead.'

The white-blond hair.

'It's me and Mum. It's always been me and Mum.'

The dents that formed just above his furrowed eyebrows.

'We don't need you. Don't want you.'

The ears—something about the ears.

'You're just some guy who used to make Mum sad. Like, abjectly sad.'

Even his smart mouth had Stevie's influence all over it.

'You lied,' Zach said next. His voice trembled. 'You helped me surf and pretended to be nice, but you lied to me.'

Not lied—he just hadn't known Zach for what he was, but now that he knew, Ethan's own mark was everywhere. There, in the boy's eyes, his wide jaw.

'You tricked me into being friends. I hate being tricked.'

The soft loops at the ends of his ear-length hair. The hairline that ran smooth across his forehead.

'I said I hate it. Why aren't you talking to me?'

The tanned skin, a color match for his own summer tone.

'Are you still drunk or something?'

That broke through. Ethan swallowed down a throat that felt like it had been packed with dry sticks. 'Probably,' he said quietly. 'I had a big day. Did you come alone?'

Zach's eyes were blown wide. Despite his defiance, he looked scared witless. 'Yes.'

'Does your mum know where you are?'

He ignored the question. 'She said you made bad choices. I'll tell you the right one. Stay away from us.'

Stevie had said he'd be confused. That he would reject the thing confusing him.

It didn't make it hurt any less.

Ethan inclined his head. He found it hard to raise it again. 'If that's what you want.' He couldn't argue—couldn't try to persuade him. Neither of them was in the right headspace for meeting in the middle.

'It is,' Zach said, even as he turned his hand, offering Hack a new spot to lick. 'And don't talk to Mum again.'

Ethan gave more of his weight to the door as he was hit by the real issue. Zach wasn't freefalling in the knowledge that he actually had a dad. No, that concept could easily elude a boy who'd been born into a single-parent family. Instead, he'd taken a mental step sideways—if his dad was alive, did that mean Ethan would get back together with Stevie?

Headlights suddenly blazed in the driveway, and a car door slammed. Then Stevie was running along the garden path, face white. 'Zach!'

Zach rounded on her, fingers balling by his sides. 'You didn't tell me!'

Her knees hit the stone patio as she reached him and grabbed his shoulders. 'Because I didn't want something like this to happen,' she said, breathing ragged. The anger darkening her eyes couldn't erase the fear. 'How dare you run away? You scared me half to death. You're grounded.'

'I don't care! He can't be my dad.' Zach's defiance vanished with those words. Tears filled his eyes. 'I don't need a dad.'

Ethan continued to hold onto the door, the only thing keeping him standing. His chest felt hollow, superfluous, a spare barrel that no one saw the need to fill.

'Zach.' Stevie darted a troubled glance at Ethan. 'I'm sorry you found out this way. But Ethan didn't know about any of this either. He didn't know you existed. He's trying to process this, just like you are. You're shocked, I know, but saying Ethan isn't your dad won't change the fact that he is.'

Zach sniffled. 'He doesn't know anything about us.'

'That's not his fault.'

At that, Zach broke down, sobbing and burying his face in Stevie's shoulder. Ethan stood there like an idiot, staring at the boy who shared his eyes and his jaw, but none of his memories.

He stared at the tender brush of Stevie's hands down the boy's back, the way his frame fit against her chest so her shoulders bent around him; stared at the instinctive way her chin tucked around Zach's shoulder, locking him even closer; and he stared at the boy's face, eyes closed and features scrunched in fear of losing his life as he knew it.

Ethan broke at the truth of their embrace.

Stevie was Zach's home.

At that, Ethan bled at how superficial his own reaction had been. He'd lamented not being able to tell Zach that he was a champion or that he was clever, that his handwriting was neat enough, that it didn't matter if a teacher looked at him sideways once in a while. Ethan had ached for all the missed opportunities to give him a high-five or trap him in a headlock while Ethan knuckled his pale hair.

What a shallow fool. He hadn't even thought about missing the chance to be the boy's home. About owning an embrace that could ease Zach's tears and lull him to sleep, because in the arms of a true parent, the world was safe.

Ethan released the door and took a step back.

He was an outsider. The only reason Zach had hunted him down was because of the authority inherent in the word 'father'. The responsibility. As if simply by being Zach's father, Ethan was entitled to claim his place beside Stevie and make decisions over Zach's life.

But no. Zach was Stevie's son.

Ethan took another step back. And another, and another. He vaguely registered Stevie's stricken gaze through the open door before he turned and staggered back toward the plastic sheeting he most definitely should not have left to answer the door.

Chapter Six

F INALLY, THERE WAS silence as Zach slept.

As always, he made no sound in sleep, rarely a movement. Over the years, Stevie had spent hours standing over his crib, hovering in his bedroom doorway, eyes trained on his ribcage, watching for the next breath, the next lift and lower to reassure her that he was still with her.

Now, she sat watching him from the edge of her bed, elbows on her knees, hands over her mouth. Her head felt two dimensional, thin, slammed flat. Her heart had taken on the extra width, plumped full and near to splitting. She prayed it wouldn't give under the pressure.

The sea moved slow tonight, so she inhaled with one crash, exhaled with the next. Keeping time with nature in an attempt to tap into its eternal fortitude, for she was going to need strength to last a lifetime.

A lifetime with Ethan, but not *with* Ethan.

How it had to be.

She'd seen his face heavy with the conviction that this couldn't work; shoulders weighted with the exclusion of an outsider. Zach had shut him out. And if Zach didn't want

Ethan in his life, then it seemed like the discussion was over before it had begun.

Except Stevie had raised Zach to be fair. She wasn't about to let up now.

Yes, he was scared, confused, and tired. The latter hadn't helped. Back at the hotel, he'd told her to promise not to see Ethan again. At her refusal, he'd clung to the hem of her singlet, stretching it as he'd sagged to his knees, hysterical, face red, cheeks wet, and she'd recognized the fear of powerlessness.

So she eased his fear and gave him power.

Said it was his choice. But he had to choose responsibly, make an informed decision, and that meant spending time with Ethan to know for sure whether to cut him out. 'Remember, you'll be spending time with him on your terms,' she'd said as he'd released her top and sat back on his shins, breath shuddering. 'Then you can decide whether or not you want to *keep* spending time with him. No one is forcing you to do anything. But you have to be grown up about this. It's a big decision.'

The argument appealed to his vulnerability. Wiping tears from his face, he'd snatched up the offer of control. 'I don't have to be nice, though.'

She hadn't pushed. But she had a solution to that one up her sleeve.

Stevie watched her son sleep until she could no longer sit up. He deserved Ethan in his life, if he wanted it, and considering they'd been getting along before all of this, she suspected that, given time, the pair would work something out. It was a father-and-son problem that would result in a father-and-son solution. Their relationship was what mattered.

Her heart squeezed against its swollen confines. The relationship between her and Ethan was secondary. If Zach felt that the control was no longer his—that Stevie had a vested interest in him liking Ethan—then he'd back away, and that wouldn't be fair on either of them.

She couldn't pursue their attraction—couldn't find out if their hearts shared the intense connection of their bodies.

It'd be better for all of them.

THERE WERE PEOPLE in Ethan's house. Their footsteps vibrated through the floor. He could smell the coffee they'd made in his kitchen; heard their hushed voices and Hack panting at what could only be a scratch on his belly. Ethan tried to roll onto his side, but his muscles jammed halfway, and he was forced to abort. He groaned, returning to his back, head set with gritty concrete.

'Morning, sunshine.'

The female voice was both familiar and unfamiliar. He cracked his eyes open and cursed his glass-paneled home as sunlight spiked into his skull.

'Keep them closed,' the woman said again, and he

obeyed. 'It's Regan. I know you remember me, because I once threatened to stuff your balls in a blender if you so much as touched my sister.'

He grimaced. 'I might have touched her.'

'Might have done more than that.'

'Why are you in my house?'

'Stevie asked us to stay with you overnight.' A male voice this time, distinctly uncomfortable. Presumably Felix. 'She wanted to make sure you were okay after…everything.'

'Okay,' he repeated, to test whether the word fit him. It didn't. He held the crook of his elbow over his forehead and attempted to open his eyes in the general direction of their voices. The pair leaned wearily against the kitchen bench.

'I've really enjoyed your lack of any form of furniture.' Regan's thumbs-up had the delivery of a distinctly different hand gesture. 'It's been a good night.'

'Then it pains me to end your stay, but you can go now.'

'Almost. Stevie called before.' Regan drained her coffee. 'Said she was on her way.'

Ethan made himself sit up. His head splintered. 'I don't need a guard,' he muttered.

'You can tell her that.'

'Zach hates me, and I'd be no good for Stevie,' Ethan said next, the truth lodging between his ribs like an untreatable blockage. 'So you can leave. There's no threat of me being in your lives.'

'Zach hates being scared,' Felix said, tone neutral. His

black T-shirt read *Change Your Password,* and Ethan felt safe assuming he was still the nerd he'd been in high school. 'Last night was his way of dealing with it.' He paused, lips quirking. 'So the threat remains.'

Ethan pushed to his feet, enduring the expected blood rush. 'Stevie really on her way?'

'Yes.' Her voice ran down his spine like gentle fingernails, and he turned to see her emerge from the wide hallway. She tossed one of two bakery bags at the others, and Felix caught it as she said, 'Thanks, guys.'

'How's Zach?' Felix passed the bag to Regan.

'Upset, grounded, and under Parker's watch,' she answered, stopping in the middle of the empty space, her blonde hair bright in the sunlight, calves bare beneath a pair of oversized shorts. The paint flecks on her chunky boots matched her white singlet, and not even his pounding head could stop the lurch of instant enchantment. Every part of him wanted her. 'But he'll turn up here soon enough,' she continued, and received a skeptical look from all three of them. 'I told him that if he wanted to hang out today, he had to come and get me.'

'You play dirty.' Regan pulled a pastry from the bag.

'With him, I play to win.'

'We'll leave you to it.' Felix ran a hand down Regan's arm. 'We've got some sleeping to do.' Despite their obvious fatigue, the pair didn't seem to resent Stevie for putting them on night watch. 'Oh.' He stilled, eyes on Stevie. 'I noticed

Ethan's painting his house.'

Her expression locked on neutral.

'I told you to tell me, Stevie.' His voice was gentle as he adjusted the slim frames of his glasses. 'Anything. Always, anything.'

'I know.' Her chin stayed level. 'But I don't need your help on this one.'

'You're supposed to be taking a break.'

She said nothing.

'You haven't had a holiday in years.'

'I went with you to Jed and Dee's wedding,' she said.

'Yeah, a whirlwind three days, because you needed to get home to Zach.' Felix didn't back down. 'I don't like this.' His gaze slid to Ethan and back again. 'On a number of levels.'

Ethan didn't either. He'd been too preoccupied by the news of having a son to consider how he'd chanced upon Stevie in the first place. 'You're painting to pay for this trip?'

Stevie's jaw ground as she met his stare. 'No.'

'I'll cover it.' Felix's stance was firm. 'Have a rest, will you?'

'Maybe she wants to do things for herself, Fee,' Regan said softly.

'And she does.' He sighed, watching his friend. 'But she knows where I'm coming from.'

Regan took his arm. 'Yeah, but maybe now's not the time.' With a pointed tug, she led him away.

Ethan remained standing, confused and hungover, in the middle of the empty room. His decency repelled the idea of employing Stevie so she could pay for a holiday that she wasn't actually taking, but her tight features said that conversation was best left alone.

For now.

'Can I get a look at the guard roster?' He swiped a hand over his hair and felt a bedraggled disaster. 'I'm going to need to plan my escape at the next change of shift.'

She arched a brow in a *very-funny* kind of way, and then extended a second bakery bag toward him. Its bulge was croissant shaped. 'We're starting over today.'

'A pastry isn't going to change the fact that Zach hates me.'

'Are you saying you don't want it?'

'Of course I want it.'

She threw it at him with a half-smile and wandered over to the ladder. It put less than three paces between them. Ethan swallowed, attraction spreading through him like a vine. Thick thorns and tough tangles and roots that latched deep—not dying out any time soon. She jumped up to sit on the second highest rung, and he noticed she'd shaken off the stress of the past few days. No more worried creases on her forehead, no downward turn of her mouth. Still serious, but she looked younger, brighter. 'I've spoken to Zach,' she started.

'You look calmer today.'

Her expression flickered. 'I guess I am.'

Calm meant her head wasn't an arena for conflicting thoughts. 'You've made a decision.'

'You're going to be his dad, Ethan. I'm making it happen.' She rested her elbow up on the top rung. Casual, easy, completely ignoring the chemistry that hummed like a lingering high note between them. Make that mostly ignoring—her gaze tripped down his chest and fell onto his crotch, before pushing back up to his face. 'So I've spoken to him. He's going to need some time.'

Ethan stared. 'After last night, I can't see time helping.'

'Trust me.' She watched him, brown gaze careful.' I told him that it's all up to him. I'm not going to make his choices. But he still ran away, and, for that, he's grounded.'

'How did he find me?'

She swore under her breath. 'That'd be my fault. I keep tabs on him with an app, but that means he can also see my location. Apparently, he'd noticed that I've been spending time here, but he assumed it was a nice bit of beach. He'd taken a screenshot so we could come back together. Last night, he figured it must have been *your* bit of beach.'

'Smart kid.'

'Don't I know it,' she muttered.

'So,' he said, having visions of Zach locked up in Lullabar. 'What does being grounded entail?'

'Random Acts of Kindness.' She smiled a little. 'I figure if I can teach my son a lesson while making a difference to the world, that's two birds with one stone, right?'

Ethan frowned. 'It's too early for me to decipher that.'

'Each act is worth a point. The severity of his naughtiness determines the number of points he has to earn off. This is the third time I've grounded him, so he knows the deal.'

Zach was only seven. 'What else has he done?'

'First time was last year when he said the F-word. I know he was just pushing boundaries, mimicking the older kids from school, but he said it with Felix around, so he couldn't get away with it. He had to earn off six points. Second time,' she said, shaking her head and not quite managing to hide her exasperation. 'Was a few months ago when I gave him permission to buy a game online, and he then proceeded to take advantage of my linked credit card to buy a series of extras. Cost me ninety-four dollars I didn't have. And before you ask, he knew exactly what he was doing.'

Ethan wasn't sure what the appropriate reaction of a parent should be, so he settled on nodding grimly.

'That was twenty points,' she said, swinging her legs from where she sat on the ladder.

'How many does he owe now?'

'Forty. He's not allowed to run away from me.' She banged her heels against a lower rung and added, 'I told him that any act of kindness toward you is worth two points.'

He lowered the paper bag, throat bitter. 'I don't want him to be nice to me because he has to be.'

'He won't. He's capable of deciding to work it off one

point at a time.' She paused. 'Okay, admittedly, I told him no swimming until he'd cleaned off all the points, so he'll want the doubles. But it's an incentive, and we need to get him talking to you. I assume.' She paused again, angling a narrow glance at him. 'You want this, right?'

Zach's warning visit wouldn't have tormented him all night if he hadn't truly wanted to get to know him. 'Yes.'

'If he comes around and loses the attitude, do you want to try to build a relationship with him?'

The thought was equal parts terrifying and magnificent. 'Yes.'

'And if you do, will you figure out a way to see him? Weekends, holidays, his birthday?'

'All the above.' And if it didn't work out, and it ended up just cards on Zach's birthday, he'd think of something proper to write, he swore he would.

'He's a good kid.' Her voice wavered when she added, 'You'll love him.'

He paused before murmuring, 'I'm sure.'

She just nodded. Not easy, he imagined, suddenly having to share her son. She was as strong as she was selfless to tuck her head down and plough forward, offering Zach in her outstretched arms. *Here's the child I raised with my tears and tenacity, while you were off becoming a better, richer person. Now that I've single-handedly managed the hardest part, feel welcome to step in and try to become his friend.*

Roles reversed, that would tear him to pieces.

'Stevie.'

She swallowed, not quite hiding her internal struggle with raised brows.

'I think I said something to you last night.'

Her legs stopped swinging. 'You said a few things.'

'About how badly I want you.'

She looked guarded. 'And you're going to tell me that was the whiskey talking?'

'I'm going to tell you it wasn't.'

Her gaze flicked down to her boots, cheeks flushing.

'I'm sorry I touched you like that.' Ethan could still feel the heat of her waist beneath his palms, the urge to spread his hands beneath her singlet, and higher. The alcohol had presumed too much.

Her hands cupped her knees. She kept her eyes down.

Unsure whether he'd drunkenly overstepped a line, Ethan said, 'All these questions about Zach and me...where do you fit in?'

Softly, she answered, 'I'm his mother.'

For a moment, Ethan focused on the pause between his breaths, that moment in time where his life hung in the balance. Unfair, that despite his similar decision, he couldn't bear that she was denying their chemistry. 'You're more than that to me,' he said.

'I heard you tell the others you wouldn't be good for me.'

'Doesn't stop me wanting you.'

'Note that we're circling back to: *How would this time be different?*'

He ran a hand over his mouth, exhaling roughly. 'I'm still working on that.'

'I'm a single mum, Ethan.' She met his gaze frankly. 'Relationships are complicated enough when there's a child involved, but you and me, we're way up on the complication scale. You're Zach's dad. If things don't work out between us, if things get messed up, it'll hurt him. And if the fallout hurts me, even a little, he'll blame you. And that'll screw up whatever bond you build with him.' She spoke with the voice of reason. And watched him with loss in her eyes. 'This is how it has to be, so that you can have a son and Zach can have a dad.'

Ethan denied this by turning toward the kitchen. He needed caffeine. A half-full plunger sat on the bench, remnants of Felix and Regan's vigil. 'Coffee?'

'No. Thanks.' Stevie changed the subject. 'I'd say we've got a couple of hours before Zach turns up.'

Ethan downed half the brew in several swallows and clunked the mug on the bench. 'As I said, I don't need a guard. You could come back later.'

'Actually.' She picked at her shorts. 'I thought we could get to know each other.'

He breathed out a laugh as he dragged the croissant from the bag. 'Really?'

'If you spend time with my kid, I want to know who you

are.'

Acknowledging that with a tilt of his head, he ate the pastry in a few swift mouthfuls. Then he drained the rest of the coffee, chased it with a glass of water and two painkillers for his headache, and said, 'I have to brush my teeth before I go anywhere near you.'

'Appreciated.' Her mouth lifted. 'I'll meet you on the balcony.'

Teeth brushed and wearing a cleanish T-shirt, he was stepping onto the balcony when his phone rang. Daniel, his assistant, spoke before Ethan could greet him.

'You have a conference call in three minutes.' Keys tapped in the background.

'What?' Ethan looked at his watch, frowning. 'Who with?'

'Disrupt Global.'

He winced. The international design firm he'd be working with on the community project. 'What do I need?'

'Just your face. It's more talks on the project. They want to nut out details for once you're in Sydney.'

'Do I call them?' he asked, and mouthed 'Sorry,' at Stevie. Unfazed, she waved him off.

'They'll call you. And please send Production sign-off on the new line.'

'Damn it.' Now he remembered his production manager asking for that last week.

'Important people routinely forget follow-up tasks.' Daniel had used this line before. It was as close as he got to reassurance. 'You are one of those people.'

A rare positive. 'Is Sarah dark on me?'

Daniel snorted. 'Sending it through with an apology wouldn't be the worst idea. And maybe one for me too, since I've had to deal with her hassling. Not easy, being your filter.'

'Sorry, Dan. Make sure I send you something nice. And remind me about the sign-off again in an hour or two.'

'Sure.' Several clicks, followed by rapid tapping. 'Oh, Ethan, a bottle of merlot. How thoughtful.'

He smiled. Daniel was invaluable. 'I thought it was two bottles?'

Another few clicks. 'My mistake. So it is.'

The call ended.

Phone held loose in his hand, he met Stevie's curious gaze. 'I've got a business call. Shouldn't be longer than twenty minutes. I'd completely forgotten.'

'That's fine.' Her lips quirked. 'If it's a video call, you might want to brush your hair.'

'Right.' A rake of his fingers reminded him of the un-kempt disaster. 'Thanks.'

When he rejoined her outside, he found that she'd opened the deck umbrella and was sitting on a chair in the shade with one knee drawn to her chest, the other tucked beneath her, gazing at the beach.

'Okay,' he said, forcing himself to sit with distance between them. Strangely nervous, he tapped his foot lightly. 'Getting to know each other. How does this work?'

She shifted to face him. 'What did you do when you moved away?'

Sighing, he leaned back and figured out where to start. 'I went to Sydney. A new city so I wouldn't be tempted to give up and drive home again. I floundered—as you saw online—until Beau dropped in and set me straight. I started my own business, which was the scariest thing I'd ever done. Something respectable, heaven forbid.'

Stevie had set her chin on her knee, watching him. 'What was the business?'

He grimaced. 'While Beau and I were fighting, I lost it completely. Said I was useless and stupid for thinking I could make myself better. That I couldn't even remember to put the bins out once a week, so how was I supposed to hold down a job? And he suggested I do that as a business; he reckoned heaps of people must forget to put their bins out, or work nightshift, or go on holiday, or are too old to pull it up and down the driveway themselves. So I started Let Us Bin It, a business that wheeled people's bins out and back in for five dollars a week.'

Her brows went up. 'Great idea.'

'I got a bit obsessed with it.' Understatement of the century. Finally, he'd had something positive that he could actually do, and it attracted all his focus. 'Did marketing, local paper interviews, and came up with all these incentives for neighbors to join in so we could get clusters of clients.' Apartment blocks and retirement villages had been winners. 'After two years, I ended up with five guys over the city—all dropouts like me—covering different regions. Wasn't a huge turnover, but I learned a lot.'

'Then what?' Stevie shifted, interested, bringing her chair closer. Her knee pressed lightly against his thigh, and his gaze dipped, running the length of her calf, narrow with lean muscle. A casual touch, comfortable. He swallowed hard, hating the way he'd grasped her last night, crossing a line— *he'd crossed many over the years—behaviorally— conversationally—always a line between people and anything unusual—he couldn't stand still—they backed away—he couldn't fill out a form—they talked down to him—he didn't remember groceries or anniversaries—they left him.*

As if labelling him socially unacceptable could change him.

'Ethan?' Stevie's voice was soft. 'I said, then what?'

He looked up as a light sea breeze gusted over the balcony. 'Then I got obsessed with something else. This is why I'm a nutcase.'

The steady stare she sent back tripped his pulse. 'Your preferred term, not mine.'

'Working in waste collection made me acutely aware of all the rubbish. So much of it, week in, week out. It got to the point where I couldn't stop thinking that, pretty soon, we wouldn't have the space for it all. I got stuck on it, you know.' Hyperfocus at its finest. Population growth was exponential. More people meant more food and more obsolete technology, and that meant more rubbish and less space for it to go. 'Some plastics don't break down in landfill. So I figured we needed to make more uses for plastic. And then I heard of this plastic-wood composite and found a small company willing to sell. I rebranded to RaftWood and built it up over a few years.'

Her frown was curious, gaze steady.

'Then I got bored of Sydney. I'd moved a couple of times, but I needed a change, and I figured I could work from wherever I wanted—the supply chain was established, and I'd hired good managers. So I moved here for a sea change. The beach has kept me occupied outside of work. So has fixing up the house.'

'But you're moving again.'

'The design firm's headquarters are in Sydney. Most of the work for the Indonesia project will be there, as well as Bali.'

She nodded, doubt creasing her forehead.

'Your turn,' he said.

'Can I see your home improvements?'

Surprised, he stood and extended an arm. 'Remember, you asked.'

She'd already seen the inside, so he took her down from the balcony and explained how the landscaped garden had originally been a slope of dirt and beach shrubs. Now the plastic-timber retaining walls held up flat stretches of grass and strappy plants of green and burgundy. She examined the wall, asking about drainage and backfill, and he answered and gestured to the façade of the house and the plastic-timber cladding laid horizontally to match the direction of the retaining walls. He then led her around to the side of the house and into the voluminous crawl space beneath.

'Oh, this is cool,' she said, moving further in.

Due to the angle of the property, the space was as big as a main room, and Ethan had transformed it around the concrete stumps: linoleum to cover the dirt, concrete render over the walls, and a workbench near the door with a cluster of bar stools tucked beneath. Vinyl couches further in, a bar fridge, and he flicked a switch so the string of Edison bulbs cast a dull amber light.

He closed the door to lock out the summer heat as she poked around.

'Tell me about after I left,' he murmured, drawing out a stool and leaning against it.

'Oh.' She turned to him, skin pale in the artificial light. 'Regan ran away. There one night, gone in the morning. That same night, Felix packed up and left his parents. I now know there was a reason for that coincidence, but not at the time.' She puffed out a humorless laugh. 'Without Regan, I followed the trend and accepted Felix's offer to move out with him.'

Ethan tried to hide his bristle, but Stevie angled her head and said, 'He's my best friend. He supported me while I was pregnant. He dealt with disapproving comments when we were in public together. He studied, worked nights, and drove me to hospital appointments. He even found me an apartment after Zach was born, not far from his place in case I needed help, but far enough that I had my own life. Zach and I would be a lot worse off if it weren't for Felix.'

Self-loathing churned through Ethan, sick and chunky. 'And I did nothing.'

'Not true,' she said quietly, moving toward him. 'You've worked hard. If you hadn't picked yourself up, this would have all gone down differently.' The air was cool beneath the house, but it heated between them, steaming, crackling. 'Because of how hard you've worked, you're in a position to accept that you have a son. To want him in your life, get to know him. And I know that you'll be an amazing dad, Ethan. I didn't know that back then, but I know it now.'

'There you go again, selfless enough to shame me.' He narrowed the distance further until the tips of his toes grazed her boots. Her body was close, taut with suppressed energy. He could sense her holding back, the same fierce restraint he had lashed around his own desire. 'You talk about how hard I've worked, yet you've brought a baby into the world and raised him on your own. You taught him sense and passion and to know his own mind. Your boy, Stevie, he's an incredible kid.'

'Ours.' Her breath was warm on his neck. 'Not a day's gone by that I haven't seen you in his eyes.'

And she looked up at him, seeing him now.

'I keep remembering that night,' he said, unable to stop himself.

The heavy look in her eyes betrayed that she did, too.

'I remember,' he said, thoughts tumbling back to his teenage bedroom, touching her, tasting her, with dawn glowing grey and impatient behind the curtains. He wanted to be doing that now, sliding his hands under her singlet, tugging it off and dragging her down onto the old couch in this secluded haven, exploring her curves, her strengths, her secrets, and loving every one of them. He wanted to—

'Ethan,' she whispered. 'You've stopped talking.'

His gaze strayed to her mouth. 'I can't concentrate.'

'Try.'

'This is me trying.'

She drew in a shaky breath. 'We can't.'

'I know.' But his need for her bound his body and stole his heart. He dared to reach out, grazing his fingertips along her cheek and drawing a tremble from her skin. Her exhale ran heat across his wrist.

'Ethan,' she said, more breath than voice.

'I just—I can't get the thought of kissing you out of my head. It's like...' He paused. 'I get distracted by periphery things, right? We all do—bright color, sudden movement, loud noise. For me, it's any color, any movement, and any noise. But the thought of kissing you, Stevie, my God, it's like a golden bird flashing right past me, singing the most arresting song. How could I possibly focus on anything else?'

Her eyes closed briefly as his fingers grazed down her neck. 'That's not fair,' she whispered. 'Have you used that line before?'

'Never.'

'Write it down.' Her eyes found his mouth and strayed. 'You'll get all the girls.'

'I don't want all the girls.'

Gloriously, her lips parted. 'That bird's not just a kiss, though, is it?'

No. 'It's all I'm asking for.'

She seemed to consider that with her body. She swayed back, as if about to refuse, but then, as her gaze travelled up his chest, his neck, to hover on his lips, the sway doubled back toward him, deciding, perhaps, that one kiss would be worth the consequent disaster. Her hand found his shoulder, and as she rose to her toes, he bent, catching her mouth with his.

The kiss started slow. Not cautious, they were well beyond that, but gentle, yes, and reverent. Like travelers moving through a sacred place, knowing they would never make a second trip in their lifetime, so every glance and gasp had to be treasured.

The heat of her lips on his.

The weight of her in his arms, her chest, hips, and mouth moving with him as he sank back against the workbench.

The taste of her morning coffee as their lips parted and tongues met.

The gasps came faster after that, but he treasured them no less. As the kiss deepened, his lust cracked, echoing through his body, spurring him on, and he chased that golden bird with everything he had. He feared he'd never catch it, not completely, no matter how far this went, no matter how many times it went there.

He was destined to want this woman until the day his blood stilled.

Greedy for her, Ethan wound his fingers through her hair, thick like his own, soft like dandelion silk, and she mirrored him, raking from his nape upward, hands closing into fists at his crown. With her elbows on his shoulders, and forearms behind, she had him locked against her. Caged in heaven, his hands found her waist and were greeted by warm cotton, taut muscle, and her tremble of desire. His muscles corded, tight with urgency as she made a small sound, a whimpered moan. Then, one of her hands dropped, sliding down between them and clamping hard.

Hot bullets of arousal shot through him.

Her palm moved, and he groaned at the pressure. He was hot all over, inside and out. Desperate to touch her, he grasped her breast, and as she tugged her singlet aside, exposing skin, he sensed it within her. The same kind of emotional and physical scrabbling that had him wanting to pull her bodily inside him and keep her there, like kissing and touching and lovemaking wasn't enough, could never be enough.

It hurt.

The force of it dug into the base of his ribcage, tearing open his fears and swallowing them whole. That he might never find a woman who accepted him as he was. That he wasn't made to have a family of his own. That he'd mess this whole thing up, screwing Stevie and Zach over in the process.

He withdrew, breathing hard. 'I shouldn't—' He groaned anew as she climbed him, arms around his neck, legs tight at his hips, and quietened him with her mouth. Gold filled his mind, and he lost himself to the chase.

It was Stevie who pulled back, God only knew how long later, palm flat on his chest, sitting on the workbench with her thighs straddling his hips, one strap of her singlet pulled down to her elbow, breathing out, 'Ethan, please.'

Assaulted by lust, he gripped the edge of the workbench on either side of her thighs. He struggled to hold steady. 'Sorry, I—'

'I know.' Her words were shaky.

'I want everything about you.'

'I—I know.' Her lips were puffy, her cheeks flushed. Her next breath was heavy, a shudder as she lowered her face, and Ethan pressed his lips to her forehead. She stiffened, startled. 'Ethan. I'm not...'

Keeping his mouth on her skin, he prompted, 'Not?'

She pulled back, her eyes tracking an unfocussed path across his collarbones. 'I'm not thinking this through.'

Whereas he was thinking what would happen if she surrendered to the raging force between them.

Couch—clothes off—greedy kisses—hot rhythm—explosive release—rest—repeat.

'God, you're giving me that look again,' Stevie murmured, words growing thick.

'You know what I'm thinking.'

'I can guess.'

'You've always done this to me.' He ached to grasp her hips, rock her hard against him. 'You must remember.'

'I do. I lived on that look.' Stevie's words nudged heat over his cheeks. Ethan dragged in a rough breath as she shifted, inadvertently rubbing the vee of her thighs against him. 'And now I remember the way you tasted.'

If her palm weren't still pressed to his chest, he'd let her remember all over again.

He did his best to focus on her conversation. 'I remember you were nervous that night.'

'I hadn't been with anyone else.'

'I hadn't been with anyone like you.'

'I remember the things you said.'

Ethan's thumbs moved, pressing into her outer thighs. Slowly, so slowly, he slid his hands up toward her hips. 'What things?'

'Something about energy. How you'd always had too

much, but you wanted mine, all of mine, and you couldn't understand how that was possible.'

Nothing had changed.

'I remember you waved goodbye.' Ethan watched her, as he had watched her in his rearview mirror. 'Mum didn't want to see me go—I left before she was home from work. Beau was passed out somewhere. But you were there. The only person who saw me off on my big adventure. You even moved into the middle of the street to wave until I was out of sight.'

'I might have cried.'

Gratified, he grasped the curve of her hips. 'What?'

She looked embarrassed. 'I thought it was stupid even as I was doing it. We hadn't dated. We weren't in love. But it was still the last time I was going to see you.'

He said, voice firm, 'I want to kiss you again.'

She didn't answer. So he tightened his grip and didn't.

'You're not thinking ahead,' she murmured.

'I told you, I can't concentrate.'

'This can't become anything. You said it yourself.'

Ethan's next breath sliced his lungs. Never had he hated his own mind more viciously than in that moment. Never wanted more violently to be normal.

He said nothing.

Stevie tugged the strap of her singlet onto her shoulder. With regret low in her voice, she said, 'Anyway, it's too risky.'

At that, risks multiplied in his head like popping corn, both sides of the argument exploding together. *Not getting to know Zach—not making love to Stevie—not taking Zach surfing—not being Zach's dad—not coming home to Stevie— not knowing a child's love—not owning Stevie's heart—not having Stevie own his—not watching Zach grow into a man— not waking to Stevie every morning—not being happy—not loving—not being loved.*

If he had neither Stevie nor Zach, he'd wither away.

Both… and he'd be the happiest man alive.

'I'm known for taking risks,' he said.

Exasperation sank her shoulders. 'Haven't you heard anything I've said?'

Stung, he abruptly stepped back.

Her brow creased, and she crossed her arms, slowly, unsure. 'Thanks.'

He looked aside, staring at the couch. Peripherally, he saw Stevie slide down from the workbench.

Quietly, she asked, 'What just happened?'

'There are phrases,' he said, jaw locking. 'Phrases I've heard all my life—from strangers, from people I care about. And you'd never said one of them, until just then.'

He looked back and met her dark-eyed look of apology. 'What phrases?'

'You're right. I guess this—' He gestured toward her, indicating the strong pull of magnetism. 'Has stopped me from thinking rationally.'

Sadness softened her gaze. 'What phrases, Ethan?'

He cleared his throat sharply. 'Pay attention. What's wrong with you? Focus. Do you even think? For someone so smart, you can be so stupid.' He paused, running a hand over his mouth. Bitterly, he added, 'Have you even heard a word I've just said?'

She ducked her head, exhaling. Her boot soles scuffed on the linoleum. After a few silent seconds, she murmured, 'Then we both have our reasons against this.'

'Yeah.'

Fuck his head to hell.

Face lowered, she moved past him. Summer heat gushed in as she opened the door, and the harsh light stabbed the back of his skull. The hangover lingered. 'For the record,' she said, washed out with the light behind her.

Ethan squinted, waiting.

'I'd never think there was something wrong with you.'

Chapter Seven

IT HAD BEEN no more than ten minutes since Zach's sullen, scowling arrival. Parker had casually declined the invitation to come inside, smart man, leaving the three of them to sit on deck chairs in the empty living space and pretend the only reason they weren't having an engaging conversation was because they were all too busy drinking their glasses of water.

Although Zach had clearly been awed by the house and the view, he hadn't commented. Although he'd succumbed to Hack's enthusiastic greeting, laughing when he copped a long lick up his nose, he hadn't asked about the dog. To do so would have gone against his resolution to ignore Ethan completely. Now, water glass empty, Zach angled his chair to face Stevie, and he starting talking with an obvious intent to exclude the man he now knew was his father.

Wary, Stevie eyed Ethan. He looked bad, sitting stiffly with darkness circling his eyes. He held his water like a lifeline, the base of the glass pressing down into his thigh. He glanced at Zach's back every so often, but mostly, he stared at the floor.

A strange sensation knotted inside her. It wasn't pity. It wasn't guilt. But with the undertones of regret, it came with the same ache.

Admiration.

This man was trying.

God, he was trying so hard. He hadn't been prepared for a son. He hadn't had months to get his head around the notion—only hours to process it before Zach had presented himself at the bar last night. And still, blindsided and floundering, Ethan wanted to see Zach. He wanted to talk to him to figure out what this could mean for their future.

Ethan wanted her, too. Stevie's gaze fell to his body, the wide spread of his knees, the curl of his fingers, and desire clasped tightly between her thighs at how he'd touched her. At first, a withdrawn kiss to respect caution, not giving himself over, and now she knew why. When he kissed properly, it wasn't really a kiss.

It was the beginning.

Heady, passionate, unapologetic—his touches had been like match strokes, the first flares of lust to get the real fire burning. As he'd skimmed her spine and shoved his hands up her legs, thumbs pressing a groove along her inner thigh, Stevie had wanted to catch flame around him. She'd been desperate to feel the weight of him, the passion, the moment of intimacy so rare. She hadn't had the energy or inclination to want that in a long time. Then he'd set her on the work-bench, his hands had found her buttons, and she'd known if she didn't stop him, he'd take her right there, and it would only take several hard strokes to have her clinging to him as she came.

Bad way to keep things uncomplicated.

So she'd stopped him, denying their attraction.

And now Zach was denying him, too.

Ethan was being blocked at every turn, and still he sat silently, patiently, waiting to be let in, if he ever would. He wasn't pushing himself on them, decreeing that as Zach's father, he *would* be a part of his son's life. No, he was leaving his involvement in their hands, and they held it without respect for just how precious that decision was.

Zach was still talking. 'And Parker said Alexia and Dee won't be back from their retreat for a few weeks, and then Dee will have to fly home, because Jed's dad is allowed to get married now, and it's happening ASAP.'

Ethan drank more water. His face tipped a little lower.

Stevie's heart turned. Her plan to get Zach warming to Ethan was failing.

'Did I tell you, Dee and Jed said I could visit them whenever I wanted?' Zach went on. 'They said I could stay in the royal quarters of the castle and everything.'

Bafflement temporarily broke through Ethan's defeat, and Stevie said, 'It's possible we know royalty by association.'

'And Jed said he was going to write a comic-book character based on me,' Zach continued, not giving Ethan the chance to question that further. 'So I'll probably have to fly over for the initial sketching.'

'Yeah, okay,' she said, placing her glass on the floor. Enough was enough. 'And what character would that be? The rude kid who doesn't understand that other people have feelings, too?'

That shut him up. He looked affronted, but unrepentant.

'So,' she said, uncrossing her legs and shifting around. 'Pity we can't go swimming.'

Zach glared.

'Well, that's not quite right.' She looked through the glass balcony doors at the turquoise water. Turning back again, she assumed a contemplative expression. 'Ethan and I could go swimming.'

The glare cut to the narrowest of slits.

'Sorry, kid,' she said without contrition. 'But I've still got you owing forty points.'

Zach's chin stuck out. 'You said if I came over, we could hang out.'

'What do you call this?'

His chin jutted further forward, and his eyes swung to where Ethan's leg was jiggling. Stevie braced herself as he flashed a look up at Ethan and muttered, 'Nice house.'

Ethan's leg stilled. 'Thank you.'

'Must be rich, huh?'

Cautious, Ethan answered, 'In a way.'

'You're so successful, but you make Mum paint your

house for you when she should be having a holiday.'

Ethan looked at Stevie, stricken.

'Sorry, my bad,' Stevie murmured. 'I've got you at forty-*five* points.'

'Mum!' Zach rounded on her. 'You can't do that.'

She leaned in, voice lowered. 'I can do whatever I want, Zachary Harvey. I know this isn't easy—we covered that last night and again this morning. But remember the part where it's not easy for Ethan either? Or for me? I need you to help. And you're doing the opposite.'

Scowling, Zach leaned back with his arms crossed. She could practically hear his mind ticking, weighing up whether snubbing his so-called father was worth being eternally grounded. Finally, he shot a swift glance at Ethan and said, 'You get to see the ocean from here.'

Apparently not worth it.

Ethan nodded, and she assumed he was playing it safe by not speaking this time—until he slid a hard look across at her, decisive, like a bolt locking into place. Or like a decision being made. Stevie's stomach sank, suspecting he was stuck on Zach's previous comment. Paired with Felix's talk this morning, he'd probably decided something for her own good.

Like no more paint job.

Irritated, she said, 'It's the sea, actually.'

Zach frowned. 'What do you mean?'

'Well, oceans don't always border land, but seas always

140

do,' she said. 'And on this coast, it's the sea.'

'So.' Zach was silent while he pieced that together. He pointed across the balcony. 'What sea is that?'

Stevie raised her brows and passed the conversation stick over her son's head. 'Ethan?'

He shifted, surprise lifting his features. 'Actually, Byron Bay is the meeting point of the Coral Sea and the Tasman Sea.'

'Huh.' Zach kept staring at the water. The tense set of his shoulders betrayed that he wasn't thrilled to be talking directly with Ethan, but he asked, 'Which is which?'

And after a pause in which Ethan sent her a glance of gratitude, he answered. His voice was low, measured, and miraculously, Zach listened. It was a blessing he enjoyed learning.

And swimming.

'Oh, cool,' he said before long, shafting an expectant glance at Stevie.

Her smile was wry. 'Back to forty points.'

His mouth twisted, pleased. He glanced once again at Ethan's agitated leg, and then up to where he played with the coin around his neck. 'You're jiggling again. Maybe we should do something.'

Ethan's hand paused. 'Like what?'

'I dunno.' He arched a brow at Stevie, gauging points. She raised a brow back, giving nothing away. 'The skate park?'

Ethan released the coin, straightening slightly. 'Blades or board?'

'Blades,' Zach answered. 'Mum's teaching me.'

'I'm no good on blades. Want to learn the board, too?'

Zach shifted in the chair, partially facing Ethan. Curiosity warred with wariness on his features. 'Is it as fun as blading?'

'Definitely. Skateboarding was created as a way to surf when there were no waves. Sidewalk surfing, they called it. So, if you liked the challenge of surfing the other day, you'll like this.'

'Huh.'

Stevie crossed her fingers by her side, holding her breath.

Zach faced Ethan a little more. 'I don't have a board, though.'

'I've got plenty. Went through a phase of making my own years ago. They're somewhere in the boxes in the garage. I'll lend you one.'

At that point, the unthinkable happened.

Zach nodded, said, 'All right,' and both guys stood. Then Zach followed Ethan into the garage without another word. Startled, Stevie looped her arm over the back of the chair, twisting to watch them go.

'No way,' she whispered. Zach hadn't even given her a point-seeking glance.

Minutes later, Ethan led the way out, talking. '...try street skating, instead. There's this awesome spot down the road, a beach lookout. It's paved and runs right off the footpath, so you've got a good lead in. There's a bench, low garden bed—concrete—and a few steps down to a second lookout. And no one really knows it's there, so it's almost always clear.'

Zach followed, holding a red skateboard, the top stenciled with a green monkey holding cymbals. He had his cool face on, lips puckered, shoulders sagging. 'Sounds good,' he said.

Stevie hardly dared to breathe. Zach was into this. Actually, genuinely into it.

Ethan met her eye as he headed toward the front hallway, and, with his back to Zach, he grinned. It was glee and fear and disbelief, all stretched into one beaming, soul-felt smile, and damned if Stevie's heart didn't falter at the sight.

'Skateboarding, hey?' She stayed sitting. It hit her then, that for the first time in her life, she wasn't sure whether she was welcome with her son. Panic stung her as the pair continued on their way. Lord, how had she not foreseen this moment? She'd given Ethan this chance, yet, suddenly, her heart rebelled against the reality.

Ethan was taking Zach out, away from her.

'Coming?' Ethan's smile didn't fade as he swiveled to face her fully, walking backwards. He raised his hands, and she belatedly saw he carried a skateboard in each. 'I thought I could teach you both at the same time.'

Relief had her sagging in the chair. *Oh, this man.*

'If you want,' he added.

Stevie gave what she hoped was a casual nod and followed.

Mindful of the fragile dynamic, she walked a few paces behind the guys. Zach couldn't feel like the third point in this triangle. She'd given him control so he wouldn't feel coerced into spending time with Ethan, and, thankfully, that seemed to be working. But she wasn't deluded enough to think he wouldn't back away shouting if Ethan and Stevie looked too comfortable together.

The moment they set their boards down, Ethan's attitude changed. Focused, enthusiastic, he admitted to getting ahead of himself earlier regarding tricks, and that they had to master coasting before anything else. Clearly in his element, he was so thoroughly distracted by teaching that any apprehension he'd felt about getting to know Zach seemed to have evaporated.

In the hours that followed, Ethan casually scattered questions alongside instructions. What else did Zach like doing, aside from skating? Was he into gaming, reading, or football? Did he like school or one subject, at least? Who did he hang out with? And Zach answered, without elaboration at first, but by the time he was able to kick and push without steering straight off the path, the pair was having a shared lament about having to learn math, because didn't everyone know it was the worst?

'Mum helps with math homework,' Zach said, raising a

shoulder, skewing his balance, and ending up on the grass. 'So it's not all bad.'

'What else does she help with?'

'Um, I have to read aloud to her most school nights,' he said. 'And I play her what I've learned on the ukulele. And we practice soccer on weekends, but I think she's taking advantage of my mad skills so that she's good enough to win her own matches.'

Stevie coasted past Ethan, feeling his gaze and the brush of his hand on her lower back. He seemed to realize too late that he'd touched her—that Zach was suddenly staring—so he pushed her on with a lunge of exaggerated vigor. 'You still play, Stevie?'

'Every second Friday night,' Zach supplied, getting back on the board and pushing himself along with fast, tiny kicks. 'It's a late match, so I stay at Felix's place. I have my own room.'

'Try gliding now,' Ethan said, watching Zach's feet. He appeared relaxed, standing back with a hand in his pocket—but his shoulders gave him away. Tense and set higher than usual. 'What do you do with Felix?'

'Play computer games. Sometimes, we go out for dinner or watch a movie.'

Stevie kicked up one end of her board and grabbed it, catching Ethan's fleeting look of disappointment. Had he envisioned doing those kinds of bonding activities with Zach? Instantly, unreasonably, resentment flashed through her.

So Ethan already imagined himself in Zach's life. Hanging out together, doing fun things. Was she going to become the boring mother in comparison? Zach could have fun with his dad on weekends, and then drag his feet back home to her rules and routine.

Horrified by that future, Stevie turned away. Down at the lookout, she pretended to take a break and stood with her back to the others. Panic fluttered her pulse. So much had happened these past few days, she'd lacked the headspace to consider how Ethan entering Zach's life could affect *her* bond with her son.

Selfish thoughts. Ethan had missed seven years of Zach's life, and he hadn't held it against her. And here she was, instinctively resenting his desire to build some kind of life with the child he'd never known.

She'd orchestrated their meeting today. They wouldn't be together if it weren't for her. She wanted, desperately, to be easygoing about this. They deserved to connect—to form a father-son relationship. She genuinely wanted that for both of them.

But simultaneously, against every reasonable thought in her head, she wanted Zach to herself. She didn't want to share him, or learn secondhand about something funny he'd said, or risk becoming redundant. *We don't have to go skating anymore, Mum. I do that with Ethan now.* And who would she spend her weekends with?

The reality of this new future had her leaning bodily against the railing, squeezing her eyes shut.

'You okay, Mum?' Zach had come up behind her.

She turned sharply, chest aching at his concerned frown. 'Yeah. I didn't want to make you feel bad, you know, because I'm picking up this skateboarding thing faster than you.'

'Mum!' He gasped, planting a hand on his chest. 'Lying is a dirty habit. I saw you stumble off the board just before.'

'All for show.'

'Oh, yeah?' He grinned. 'I challenge you to a skate off.'

Smiling, she dropped her board and set her foot down. 'You're on, baby.'

And her fears abated, overshadowed by activity. By the end of the afternoon, Zach earned off all forty points. There were only a handful of moments when she saw him pause as he looked at Ethan, uncertainty clear on his face, as if he'd realized afresh that Ethan was somehow his dad. So she complimented his glide or punched him lightly in the shoulder, and he'd grin at her and return to the safety of the immediate situation.

When the sun became unbearable, they called it quits.

'Mum,' Zach asked, tugging up his shirt to wipe his face. 'Are we driving back?'

'Walking.'

He turned to Ethan. 'Can I borrow the board?'

Ethan nodded, features wide in earnest. 'Yeah, of course.'

'Mum, can I go ahead?'

Frowning, she eyed the quiet footpath, so different to the city streets of Melbourne. 'Listen for cars reversing, and don't go on the road. I'll catch up.'

'Cool.' Then, half-turned away, he said, 'Oh, Ethan?'

Stevie stopped breathing, wondering if this was it.

Ethan ran the back of his hand over his forehead and said, 'Yes, mate?'

'Sorry I yelled at you last night.' His head was down, fingers picking at the edge of the board.

Stevie's heart ballooned and Ethan's brow creased, moved by the apology but clearly trying not to show it. 'That's all right.' He hit the perfect note of serious yet casual. 'It's been a bit full-on, hey?'

'Yeah.' Zach scuffed the pavement. 'Wanna go to the skate park after dinner tomorrow? I don't want to miss the program again, because Vik said it was circus stuff and I'm good at balancing. But I could show you what Mum's taught me on blades. If you want.'

Zach wanted to see Ethan again; he wanted to share a part of himself. Rollerblading, a part that Stevie had made possible. That unreasonable fear gathered between her lungs, tight, pinching, catching on each breath. She didn't know whether she could handle this.

She had to handle this.

Ethan tucked his board under his arm and said, 'I'll be there.'

Zach nodded before setting off, arms out wide, pushing, gliding, stumbling onto the nature strip.

Side by side, Stevie and Ethan watched him go. Silent, struck by the magnitude of the past few hours and the promise embedded in Zach's final invitation.

'Hey, Stevie,' Ethan said in a half-whisper, and then turned to her, grinning. Her pulse stuttered at his joy. As confusing as everything was, she still yearned to kiss this man where he stood. 'He invited me to the skate park.'

She managed to smile. 'I know.'

'I feel like—' He paused, shaking his head. 'There's nothing like this feeling.'

She almost pressed a hand over the pinching in her chest. Nothing at all.

Striving for indifference, she said, 'I'll see you tomorrow,' and passed him her skateboard.

He took it, frowning. 'About that.'

Her chin lifted. Here it came, as if she needed another challenge.

'You working for me isn't right, Stevie.' He shifted, angling his broad shoulders toward her. She could smell him, a masculine mix of sunscreen and physical effort that left her hormones gasping. 'Things have changed since I thought this job would be a cool way to catch up. I say no more painting, but I'll give you the full amount quoted. I'm not going to shortchange you on this. What do you think?'

'I think no.'

Ethan sighed. 'Yeah, I figured.' His gaze flickered up the street before locking back on her, steady as ever. 'And I get your need to earn your own way. But look at it from my view—I'm setting the mother of my son to work on my house because she needs the income to raise him. Surely, you can understand how that makes me feel like a complete arsehole.'

Her stomach twisted. When he said it like that. 'It's too early for you to get involved financially.'

'I get that, too. And I know money is a sensitive topic.' He brought himself closer, tilting his head down and lowering his voice. She swallowed, resisting the mouth that had devoured hers so beautifully hours before. 'But I've contributed shit all to your life—and Zach's—and that's sensitive to me.'

'Then be there for him.' She glanced down the street. Zach was about five houses away, coasting with knees bent and arms wide. 'That's what he needs. Because I'm not taking your money unless I've earned it.'

'Damn it, Stevie.' For a second, she thought she'd won. Then, he said, 'What's the money for? School books? Uniform? New shoes? I'll buy that for him instead. My purchase, my money. Not giving it to you. Just stop working for me, all right? I'm not the only one who's uncomfortable about it.'

'No.' She turned, cornered, glaring at the beach. 'Look, this job isn't for Zach. It's for me. I'm putting myself through uni, okay? I've enrolled in an Associate Degree in Engineering. It's a back pathway to get into the full degree. I have to buy this specialized software and textbooks, and with the admin fees and this trip on top of it all, I need some extra income. That's what this job's for. Not Zach.'

Ethan had straightened beside her, clearly startled.

'I haven't told Felix yet, because I might fail or find it too hard, and he's so damn smart. But Zach and I have talked about it, and he's okay with it. He said it'd be cool if we do homework together.' She watched Ethan run a hand along his jaw, no longer having a card to play. 'And since I'm absolutely not going to accept your money for myself—I'll see you tomorrow.'

Reluctant acceptance settled over his features.

'Okay then,' she said. That decided, she turned to go.

'Stevie.'

Her name spoken in his voice resounded inside her, a warm echo. She looked back at him, and her breath faltered. Sunlight stuck to his hair like toffee, while his gaze stuck to her.

'If you're serious about us staying apart—and you should be, I'll never be good for you—you've either got to stop being so amazing or let me win this round. Because being alone together doesn't seem to lend us the strength to resist.'

Her breath faltered at the look in his eye. That look. She would stay away from him if she could, but she had a different choice to make.

Put physical distance between their chemistry or put professional distance between their personal lives.

And today, right now, she didn't know how she'd handle Ethan's only place in her life being Zach's dad. It confused her, hurt her, and turned her into someone she didn't want to be.

She needed the job between them. Just for a few more days.

'Last chance,' he murmured, gaze dropping to her mouth. 'Please.'

'I'll stop being so amazing.'

'I was angling for you letting me win this round.'

'No such luck.' She turned after Zach. 'Until tomorrow.'

She heard his pained exhale and the words, 'Bad idea.'

Yeah. But it was the best she had.

Chapter Eight

'LET'S REWIND TO when you said she was my One.'

Ethan jogged lightly on the spot, bare feet lifting and landing on manicured grass. The peaceful grounds of Vik's yoga retreat sat in near silence around them, the rising sun yawning light across the minimalist timber structure, tree-shadowed garden, and forested hills beyond. Half a dozen guests lunged at the far end of the grass, stretching through the movements of a sun salutation.

Vik had appeared on Ethan's doorstep before sunrise, ushering him to the retreat—a common occurrence when his friend suspected tension overload. Vik had spent the past half-hour sitting beside him in the lotus position, eyes closed, undisrupted by Ethan's form of meditation. The jogging had been Vik's idea when Ethan had first moved to Byron Bay and attended a workshop, desperate for a calmer mind. Unusual, yes, but a fidgety body wasn't conducive to relaxation, and Ethan's thoughts were rarely as settled as during his morning runs. So jogging on the spot it was.

Now, Vik opened his eyes. 'Was I right?'

'You were unfair to say it.'

On a long exhale, his friend said, 'Because I was right.'

'Because now all I can think about is having her in my life. And that's not possible.' He kept moving. 'You've sentenced me to pointless chaos.'

'Ethan.' Vik ran his hands along his thighs and rested them on his knees. 'You have to learn to put the things you want above the things you fear might happen.'

'There's no *might* about them.'

'You're precognizant?' He feigned mild surprise.

'I'm trying to be pragmatic.'

'Why isn't it possible?'

'Because I've never stayed in one spot long enough to trust that I can,' he said, number one on a very long list. 'I get bored, you know that. Leaving a family because of restlessness would be sheer pricksville, but if I stayed, I'd probably make their lives even worse.'

'Want to know the funny thing?' Vikas had closed his eyes again.

'Only if it's actually funny.'

His mouth curved. 'You get bored because you don't grow roots. There's nothing meaningful to hold your interest. And you don't grow roots because you're scared you're going to get bored and need to leave.' A parrot pinged in the trees. 'Catch twenty-two.'

Ethan exhaled long and hard, staring at the grass until it became a green blur.

That had literally never occurred to him before.

'Okay,' he said, hauling himself back on track. 'Let's say I could stick around. Doesn't change the fact I'm a nutcase. I'd drive her—both of them—crazy.'

'Let's dream a little. Tell me how your ideal companion would deal with you.'

With effort, Ethan eased Stevie out of his head and envisioned a faceless form. 'She'd have to be independent—not reliant on me for everything, in case I forget or get distracted.'

But he'd make up for it with surprises, dinners, dates. He'd be unreliable, but spontaneous.

'She'd be easygoing. Open-minded. Tolerant.'

She wouldn't stick him in a box and seal him up with preconceived ideas.

'Curiosity would be nice,' he said, shifting to a springier section of grass. 'She'd want to know what I'm excited about or interested in. Or at least ask. I'd like to share my ideas.'

Try as he might, the faceless image of his ideal companion kept taking on Stevie's features.

'Active,' he listed next, strangely helpless. He wasn't manipulating these traits to match her; he swore he wasn't. 'She'd understand the need to go for a run or spend an hour or two at the gym. My energy wouldn't be an issue, because she'd be active too.'

Realization was washing over his resistance, forking around the truth Vik had spoken.

'She'd want to have a family with me.'

He sighed, stopped jogging, and met his friend's knowing gaze.

'She'd be Stevie.'

ETHAN WASN'T HOME when Stevie arrived. Instead, another note was stuck to the unlocked front door. *Dragged out, home later. Help yourself to kitchen. Zach kind of likes me! E. x*

Heart in her mouth, Stevie gave Hack a rowdy greeting, helped herself to Ethan's coffee, and set up in the sunny back room.

Zach kind of liked him.

True, and terrifying, that fact had kept Stevie awake all night.

The previous afternoon, Zach had talked non-stop—about skateboarding, surfing, and superheroes. After a quick google, he declared himself Rocket Racer and begged to go out skateboarding again when it wasn't so hot. So they did, followed by a group walk around town, where he'd balanced on every curb and raised garden bed they passed, arms wide and feet flying. He hugged strangers' dogs. He groveled for ice cream. He ran ahead in a charge of energy, and then dashed back, cheeks flushed, eyes shining.

He was on a high.

He had a dad.

'Mum,' he'd said, trying Felix's iced coffee. He pulled a face and clasped his hands for a mouthful of Regan's chocolate milk. 'Can we buy a house and live here?'

Stevie's gut balled. Felix looked at her sideways, straw in his mouth. 'What about your friends?' she asked, faking interest in a beach-chic furniture window display. She hated every piece.

'They can visit.'

She turned. 'You want to live near the beach, do you?'

His shoulder lifted. 'Gotta be lucky to live where two seas meet, right?' And he'd looked up at her, tawny eyes steady. 'We could do with luck, Mum.'

A lump rose, hard, in her throat.

Could they?

'Too hot here, man,' Felix said casually, nudging Zach ahead with his foot. 'I wouldn't visit you.'

As Zach moved ahead again, Felix's hand moved lightly across Stevie's shoulder blades. 'You okay?' he murmured, and Regan peered around him to listen.

No. But how could she admit to wanting Zach and Ethan to form a bond, while simultaneously not wanting Ethan to change a single part of their lives?

'It's all happening so fast,' she'd said under her breath.

Fast, like rising water.

No matter what happened from here, the life she had built with Zach would change. A simple life, yes, and tough at times, but it was theirs. That unprecedented fact had kept her up late into the night, sitting on the hotel room balcony and staring powerlessly at the dark waves until dawn poured cream across the sky. She had to roll with the punches. God knew she'd done it before, but it didn't ease the impact.

Or the sleep deprivation this morning.

Stevie helped herself to a second coffee, a toasted slice of Ethan's bread, then cranked up the music and got to work.

She had just finished painting the main living space when Hack trotted to the internal garage door, tail wagging. Pulse spiking at Ethan's imminent arrival, she knelt to rest the roller in the paint tray as he stepped inside and immediately hunkered down to greet the boxer.

His gaze flicked up, and he smiled to find her at eyelevel. 'Morning.'

Stevie nodded, watching as Hack slid onto his back, rolling delightedly under Ethan's palm. She melted a little as Ethan made happy hello noises—she'd always found something gorgeous about a man greeting a pet. It showed openness for affection, and consideration for the creature's delight when it could so easily be overlooked. This job had put Stevie in a lot of people's homes—in their personal spaces. She knew the truth in judging people by how they treated their inferiors—because as a laborer, many people deemed her as beneath them.

She'd been ignored and spoken about as if she weren't in the room. She'd been ordered around, reprimanded, and had arrived for jobs across town to find no one home. Most notable was when she'd been watched for several hours by a woman talking on the phone, drinking coffee and eating biscuits, without once speaking to Stevie or offering the use of the kettle. Yes, Stevie was being paid to do a job, but how could some people believe that lessened her value as a human?

Stevie stood, slowly.

Ethan didn't. Not once, since she'd started this job, had he acted like she was less because she had a paintbrush in her hand. Appreciation knotted with her admiration.

His head might be chaos, but he was sense and sanity in the ways that mattered.

Her gaze travelled over him. A black singlet exposed his toned, muscled arms, and loose, cotton pants fell over his bare feet. He looked casual, sexy, and energetic. A man who spent free time *doing* rather than *being*.

Like her.

Ethan straightened, rolling his shoulders, and Hack trotted off outside. Wincing slightly, he stretched an arm across his chest, head tilting.

'You okay?' she asked, aware she was standing and staring.

'I spent the morning meditating at Vik's retreat. Then he ordered me to stay for yoga while he went to meet the circus instructors. He wanted me to calm my mind.'

'Did it work?'

His arms relaxed. 'He'd say it worked.'

'And you'd say...'

'I now have different things to think about.'

She nodded, pretending to understand as he moved toward her.

'Sorry I haven't been here this morning.' His gaze moved across the walls, and his closeness sent a stream of impulses through her body. Besieged by attraction, she swayed toward him.

Fighting to hold strong, Stevie gathered up the roller and paint tray. 'I'm about to move to the hall.'

'I'll help.' He lifted the half-empty paint tin and her lukewarm coffee, then straightened, watching her with an unusual expression. Not the look that stripped her of appetite in high school, but one step more devastating. Concentrated levels of awareness and desire, unfiltered, undiluted, and something she hadn't seen in his eyes before, something that aimed right for her heart and struck sure and true.

Hope.

Flushing, she dropped her gaze and led the way into the hall. 'Zach liked yesterday, you know. He told Felix and Regan about how cool you were, teaching us to skateboard.' Ethan's bare feet were soft in her wake, his presence like a magnetic pressure against her spine. Her back ached for him to close in behind her, arms locking around her middle and holding her tight against him. She set the equipment down, shooting a sidelong glance to where he was lowering the paint tin. Back straight, one knee on the floor, his pants sitting low on his hips and pulling tight across his muscled butt.

Stevie closed her eyes, seeking inner strength.

Maybe she should try yoga.

As they returned to the living room, Ethan asked, 'Is this PJ Harvey?'

She nodded at the singer's husky voice.

'Did she inspire Zach's middle name?'

Surprised, Stevie said, 'Yes.'

'And Zachary?' he asked as they both reached for the unopened paint tin. Stevie tensed, too aware of the wide span of his hand, the bare skin of his arms, the merciless lure of his casual clothes. The impulses intensified, demanding all of her resources to fight and leaving her without basic function, like breathing or moving or the ability to take her eyes off him.

Ethan drew back, mistaking her stare as a challenge, and gesturing for her to carry the tin. He moved for the ladder instead.

Softly, she said, 'I just like the name.'

His smile was gentle. 'So do I.'

Her insides looped as they returned to the hall. 'What would you have named him?'

Ethan frowned beside her. 'I've never considered kids' names before.' Ladder down and latched safely, he regarded her strangely. 'But if I'd been there,' he said, pausing with a small frown. 'If I'd been there, and you'd suggested Zach...I'd have loved it.'

Stevie missed a breath; fought hard to catch the next.

'Everything you've done,' he said, facing her. 'I love it.'

Unable to speak, she nodded and set to work.

His appreciation made her insides feel jumbled, as if her heart had sank to her stomach, and each beat was exposed, unprotected by bone. Not safe from him, not when he spoke like that.

They worked in silence. With the whole house sanded and prepped, she painted the hall ceiling and he started on the walls. Every time her attention drifted to Ethan, she saw Zach's father. She saw the man who made her skin burn and body ache. She saw the man who could change everything forever. A good man. A lover. And a threat. So she clenched her teeth, thinking and feeling too much, and got back to work.

'You okay if we keep doing the get-to-know-each-other thing?'

Stevie jumped and shot him a hesitant look. Ethan was pressing a roller into a tray, collecting eggshell paint. His gaze was on her.

She braced. 'Okay.'

He glanced down, adjusted his grip, and met her eye again. 'Pretend it's not wrong to want anything. What do you want?'

She stared. Not wrong to want anything? A dangerous concept. 'A sleep-in.'

He smiled, head tilting. 'I want six answers.'

'To be an engineer,' she said, another easy one as she climbed down the ladder. Aware of the irony, she added more paint to her roller and shot him a defiant glance.

Ethan waited, smile gone, gaze steady.

'More time.' Always more time. 'For grocery shopping, and cooking, and playing with Zach, and driving him around, and working, and sleeping in. And soon, for studying.'

At her hesitation, he held up a hand with three fingers raised.

'Sometimes,' she said, speaking through pain that felt a lot like failure, 'I want help.'

The roller ended up loose by his side. A thick drip landed onto the plastic sheeting. 'Help with what?'

'Everything I just listed.'

His solemn look didn't judge her. It understood.

She moved on. 'I want...' Suddenly six answers seemed like so few. 'For people not to think there's something wrong with me.'

Why are you working this job, sweetie? You could be in admin.

Or when the client was male: *Here, you'll hurt yourself. Let me help.* As if she didn't carry ten-liter paint tins with a ladder under her arm every day.

Ethan put the roller in the tub, frowning. Wiping his hands together, he approached, and her lungs emptied at the intense look in his eye. 'How could people think there's something wrong with you?'

Stevie chucked her own roller down, ignored the question, and moved on to number six. 'I want to have not said that phrase to you.' The admission came out small, her thumbs hooked self-consciously into the low sides of her overalls. 'I've been hurt by people saying certain phrases my whole life, too. And I hate that I'm one of those people for you.'

He was in front of her now, eyes searching her face. Every nerve in her body reached for him, stretching, desperate for his touch. 'Tell them to me.'

She strove for indifference. 'When I was younger, it was things like: Are you a boy or a girl? You'd look really pretty in a dress. Why don't you grow your hair?'

His brows rose. 'Did you ask why they conformed to gender stereotypes?'

'Strangely, I didn't think of that at age seven.'

Lips curving faintly, he said, 'Just so you know, I've always been mad for this hair.'

Her face warmed. 'I remember.'

Smile fading, he reached out and ran a hand through her short spikes. His fingertips grazed her scalp, sending thrills cascading down her spine, and she breathed in, copping a lungful of paint fumes and masculinity. Attraction tightened her body. Squeezed her muscles. Released a hard pulsing between her thighs.

Voice low, he asked, 'What phrases do you hear these

days?'

She swallowed. 'Do you dress like that because you want to be a boy? What sport do you play? Do you have a girl-friend? Oh, you're straight, so does that mean you're the dominant one in the relationship?'

It was a miracle she hadn't been driven to violence.

'I know I'm different,' she said, eyes half-closing as his hand settled at the back of her neck. 'And there are people who have a much harder time than I do, God help them. But damn it, my sexuality is no one else's business.' She was getting worked up, despite his touch. 'Why does difference automatically mean I have to explain myself to strangers?'

'Hey.' His free hand unhooked her fingers from her overalls and laced them through his. Raising them to his mouth, he kissed the back of her hand. Gently, from over her knuckles, he said, 'Screw, 'em.'

She breathed out a laugh. 'And then there were the phrases I heard while I was pregnant. I mean, during my *teenage pregnancy*. The world rallied together to tell me that I sucked. Your life is over, they said. You've thrown away your future.' Unable to meet Ethan's gaze, she looked at the wall over his shoulder. 'Only stupid girls get pregnant in high school.'

He didn't move.

'I believed them,' she murmured.

She heard his bitter exhale; felt the culpability in his mo-tionlessness. 'I'm so sorry, Stevie.'

Raising a shoulder, she looked down. Bad idea. Ethan stood so close; one little lean would have her kissing the exposed skin above his neckline. Paint smeared the hem and the pocket of his summer-weight sweatpants. His bare toes were a sun-kissed tan upon the wooden floor.

She met his gaze, taking the conversation back a step. 'Not once have you treated me like I'm different.'

'Not because I'm perfect.' His voice was rough. 'In high school, your clothes and interests were irrelevant. I just wanted you.' His smile was tentative, seemingly too aware of what she'd endured because of their attraction. 'I had pretty straight-forward goals back then.'

She had to ask. 'And now?'

His attention slipped to where her breasts hid beneath her singlet and heavy-duty overalls. His fingers tightened on her. 'I'm getting some overlap.'

Throat thick with aching, she nodded.

Ethan's thumb ran over her knuckles. 'We should get back to painting.'

'Okay,' she murmured.

'Okay.'

They both held still. Two oppositely charged bodies, destined to collide. So close, his breath moved the hair at her temple. Her ragged exhale shuddered between them.

'You didn't respect me, back then,' he said, voice quiet.

Shame flushed her cheeks. 'I wanted to.'

'You—came to me anyway.' His eyes were dark, and his

face sank fractionally closer. 'You let your body take control.'

'I don't regret it.'

Softly, 'Would you do it again?'

She heard the real question. 'I respect you now, Ethan. It wouldn't be the same.'

At that, his lips pressed against the back of her hand again, once, twice, before traveling along her knuckles, openmouthed kisses that left her skin wet. He uncurled her grip and kissed the grooves between her fingers, her palm, down her wrist. Then, smoothly, he lifted his head and used his hold on her neck to draw her to him.

She didn't fight it, didn't want to. She surrendered to his mouth, to the higher power between them, giving in to a wealth of sensual opulence—richness in the smooth heat of his skin and fortune in the lavish depths of his kiss.

Ethan jumped under her palms and kissed harder, hungrier. Hands on her arse, he grabbed, lifted, urged her legs around his waist and he stepped once, twice, propelling her back against the painted wall. Touch dry, but it was unlikely to take full-body pressure. What the hell.

They'd do another coat.

Ethan's body crowded her, a surging press of hips, chest, and shoulders—and dazedly, she touched every part she could reach. His hands clutched the back of her thighs, gripping tight as his mouth covered hers again. Lush and thorough, the kiss poured the taste of him through her with the weight and worth of liquid gold, and everything within her pitched forward, desperate to pass between his lips and form a worthy part of him.

Ethan's grip loosened, and she moaned as the vee of her thighs slipped to press over his erection. She had his singlet off between one ragged inhale and the next.

'Can we do this?' His voice was strained in her ear. 'I don't—if you're not—'

'Please.' Full-body need had cleared her head. Nothing could contradict this. Her spine bent, arching as she ground against him. 'I can't think.'

His lips stretched, smiling, against her neck. 'I'm contagious.'

'Yes.'

And he was the cure.

'Get these off.' He moved a hand to her overalls. Unsteadily, she unclipped the straps, breath coming fast. Several men had filled her bed since Ethan, but none had triggered such acute lust. She'd forgotten how it stung, tightening her skin like a hot yet glorious sunburn. How it raised her heart to an almost panicked pulse. How it overwhelmed rational thought with emotional excess.

The straps fell away. Freed, she peeled off her singlet. Ethan discarded her bra, and then he was cupping her breasts, thumbs flicking over her nipples, pressing harder, shoving them higher. Stevie's head dropped back as his mouth replaced thumb, setting sparks of pleasure showering through her, falling in a hot heap low in her abdomen.

Her body was shaking. Anticipation begged for him inside her.

'Ethan.' She gasped. This was all she wanted. 'I don't have…I don't—'

'By the bed.'

He inched back, and she landed on her feet. The overalls fell over her hips, and she kicked off her boots. One hit the ladder. Then she and Ethan collided again. Within seconds, she was back around his waist. Stevie busied herself with the firm muscle on his shoulder, kissing, suckling, as he set off toward the mezzanine. By the top, his breathing had roughened.

'Sure?' he managed, halting before the bed. 'You're really sure?'

'Yes.'

Sunlight glared down from the glass-paneled ceiling, revealing the messy twist of covers on his bed, the pillow on the floor. Ethan tipped her onto the mattress, standing back to slide off his sweatpants and reach into the bedside drawer. Stevie shifted against the sheets, knowing this would change everything. The light exposed his nakedness, every beautiful inch of it, and when his hot gaze raked over her figure, energy thrummed between them like a tight cord plucked into vibration.

This wasn't a quick hookup to clear their heads. This was the missing link from their future. Stevie and Zach. Ethan and Zach.

Stevie and Ethan.

He came down beside her, and she turned, touching, into the line of his body. The rounded strength of his shoulders, the powerful cut of his arms, the muscle-plated stomach. The warm metal of the coin around his neck, the soft underside of his jaw, and the almost nervous lines of his face.

She stilled, tracing the crease between his brows. 'Are you sure?'

His smile was wary. 'It's just—last time.'

Her fingers found his hand clutching the condom. 'This is different.'

'Maybe I should use two?'

She smiled, shaking her head as she rose onto her elbow and kissed his collarbones. Here was a man she'd craved since adolescence and only now had time to properly devour. She wanted to use his breathing as a guide, savoring the places of hitches and gasps. She wanted to find where her mouth fit best, the curves and dips and edges. Wanted to put her scent on his skin and consume his every thought.

Before she could have her way, Ethan rose up beside her, his usually honeyed eyes burnt dark. His fingers gently grazed her shoulder before he pushed her more firmly back onto the mattress. 'You stay here.'

'But I want—'

'You're better at staying still. Let me move.'

Trumped, Stevie stayed as Ethan moved down the bed,

attention locked on her body as his hands explored. Gathering her breasts, fanning over her waist, brushing over the dip of her belly button. Her skin seemed to stretch beneath his touch, straining to remain beneath his palm. The tug only intensified when he moved on, a torturous ache, and by the time he reached her hipbones, she couldn't bear it any longer and sat up to draw him close.

'Stevie,' he murmured, surprised, pausing to surrender to her embrace. His hand brushed down her spine, leaving it straining like the rest of her.

He kissed her jaw, and her heart swelled. 'Please.'

'What, darling?'

Simply, she admitted, 'I want you everywhere.'

He grew still, gaze tracking her face. Softly, he said, 'All right.' Then he was easing her back once more, keeping an arm spread up her sternum, his fingers toying with the hair behind her ear, and she turned her face into his hand, clutching his forearm against her chest.

Better this way, having him closer.

Several heartbeats passed before she realized Ethan had gone still, hovering over her abdomen. Caught by the sight of her faded stretch marks, it seemed, and she watched regret pull his eyes closed. Marks from a time he would never get back, physical reminders of the son he'd never see borne. Then he swooped down, pressing his lips to her stomach with such gentle reverence, Stevie was left blinking back tears.

Moving lower, Ethan's hands passed over her hips to map the curve of her bottom, before sweeping smoothly back over her thighs and nudging them apart. Arousal kicked her hard when his palm cupped her, thumb placed just so, and she hung on a long breath as he stroked her center, once, twice, before pushing inside. Slick, sweet sensation pinned her to the mattress. His fingers moved, slow and seductive, and the straining of her skin was suddenly nothing compared to her desperate need for Ethan's touch within. Everywhere, all at once. She was tense with it, shuddering, fingers grasping the sheets, gasps catching in her throat. Such heavy pleasure, reaching far beyond muscle and into memory.

Ethan Rafters, her lover of this lifetime.

She moaned, and his eyes met hers, hazy with lust.

'Please,' she gasped, and he shifted, shoulder dipping, elbow brushing the inside of her knee, and then he was stroking her deeper, and, *God,* his mouth was closing over her, intensely hot, and the pressure inside her built so rapidly that she clutched at the sheets and arched her back and pressed her eyes shut against the blue summer sky.

'You gonna wait for me?' he murmured, breath sending heat across her stomach. His other hand was at her breast, toying, pushing, indulging.

Her hips lifted as he stroked her again. 'I can't.'

So he withdrew, the sex in his eyes burning a path along her body, and she sat up to meet him once more, clutching his neck, her kiss openmouthed and urgent. A ball of need had been gathering inside her, tightening, aching to burst for him, all for him.

It hadn't been like this last time. She'd let him lead, not knowing what to do.

Now, she straddled him where he knelt. Ethan made a greedy sound at the back of his throat, hands running down her sides, and she knew the desire ripening inside her was anchored deeper than hormones. She respected him, admired that he'd pulled himself out of dereliction despite the chaos in his head. How could anyone resent his failings when he constantly strove to be a better version of himself?

'You're exceptional,' she murmured, kissing the sensitive skin behind his ear.

'I have my moments.' He snatched up the packet from the mattress, chest rising and falling, features heavy and hungry and beyond words beautiful.

Stevie took the packet from him. Deliberately, she protected him with a tight grip, and murmured over his reaction, 'Every moment.'

The small frown that flickered between his brows eased as she settled over him and sank down. Instantly, the need inside her tightened, glowing white, hot. So close, so soon—she'd needed this for days. Needed him. Ethan hooked an arm around her waist, drawing her fully against him, and her soul flamed as their naked skin pressed together. Stomach to stomach, breasts to chest, and nose to nose: he held her so near, there was nowhere to look but into the stare where all this started.

Stevie shuddered as he pulled her hips down again, mouth catching her moan as he filled her. His tongue sought hers, matching their slow rhythm as his strokes became longer, deeper. Pleasure spilled inside her, up and over, with each clutch and drag. They were sweating. The bedding had fallen to the floor. Their breathing drowned out the crash of waves and call of gulls outside.

'This feels right, doesn't it?' He breathed the question across her cheek.

Right...and so intense the physicality threatened to consume her. 'Yes.'

'I've never wanted anyone like I want you.'

'Yes,' was all she could manage before he kissed her again, long, luscious, her tension building with each stroke, leading her higher. Then he angled his hips, hitting differently, surging closer to the tight ball high inside her. She whimpered as he touched it, pushed into it, and broke it apart with hard thrusts, filling her with an orgasm so pure and hot and thrumming that she clamped around him and knew nothing but light.

She couldn't speak, couldn't make a sound as ecstasy devoured her.

Then she fell limp in his grasp, forehead pressed into his shoulder, dragging in air.

'Can we switch?' His voice was edgy, close.

Too lost to answer, she nodded and ended up on her

back. With one arm holding her hips high, the other gripping the headboard, Ethan knelt between her thighs and rocked into her, nearing the end of his own race. Gasping, heart flying, Stevie pushed back until his movements roughened and the bedhead creaked under his white-knuckled grip. His rough groan of release was so unbearably sexy that a second wave of pleasure crashed over her, gentler, sweeter, and she knew in that moment Ethan was the only man who could love her like this.

He collapsed over her, and her skin rejoiced.

Her heart cowered.

There would never be anyone else.

Chapter Nine

S TEVIE LASTED ROUGHLY twelve seconds before the tears started.

Emotion heaved inside her, hauled to the surface by the rush of hormones. Defenses lowered by euphoria, she was left vulnerable and open to the onslaught. Ethan rested over her, softly kissing her neck, his fingers trailing idly along her side, ignorant of the tears drowning her eyes, slipping quickly down her temple and into her hair.

She tried to contain it. Clamped her jaw tight, inhaled slowly through her nose. But his tenderness fed the guilt inside her, affection she didn't deserve, until a traitorous breath shuddered in her chest.

Ethan stilled. He pushed up to his elbows, frowning at her brimming eyes. Concern had him asking, 'Are these happy tears?'

Horrified at herself, Stevie turned her face aside. A sob came from the pit of her belly.

Exhaling roughly, he slid out of her. 'Not happy.'

Stevie curled up with her back turned as he moved to the edge of the bed. There was the soft scrape of tissues leaving the box, a quiet moment, and then he was easing over her and tucking himself around her, wrapping her up in his body, refusing her attempt to shut him out.

'Hey,' he whispered, running his fingertips over her scalp.

Eyes too full, she tilted her face down as guilt tore her in two. One half never wanted to let him go. The other couldn't bear being this close. A pitiful series of sobs filled his confused silence.

'Can you tell me what's wrong?'

She shook her head.

'Can't or won't?' His touch focused on her nape, massaging tender muscle.

Both. She managed to halt the sobbing, but her vision still swam. 'I can't stop thinking.'

Ethan's body closed tighter around her, a clam protecting its pearl. 'I know the feeling.'

She sniffled, breaking at his earnest gaze. 'I don't want to think like this. It's not fair on you.'

Caution clouded his features. The tendons in his neck flexed as he swallowed. Several long seconds passed before he said, 'You're thinking you don't want to be with me.'

Her inhale shook, light and unsatisfying. She breathed deeper. 'I—do.'

'You know Zach won't want it.' Another guess, equally stricken.

'He won't. But that's not it either.' Ethan deserved the

truth. Reaching into the conflict inside her, she yanked out the ugliest thought she'd had in years. Voice small, she said, 'A part of me doesn't want you to be with Zach.'

He jerked. Lay rigid around her, as if tension could stop that wound from bleeding. He spoke into the silence. 'You're going to shut me out.'

The devastation in his voice curdled her pride. 'No. Of course not.'

Ethan's eyes darted back and forth across the sheet. 'I'm not good enough for him.'

'No, that's not—'

'I've never been good enough for him.' He uncurled and sat up, sudden, stiff. The thick of his thumb pressed between his brows. 'My dumb head jumped too far ahead, and I believed it.'

'Ethan.' She sat up, grabbing his wrist and pulling his hand down. Of course he'd think this, his mind running where she'd inadvertently pointed. 'I want you to be Zach's father.'

Disbelief held his spine straight. 'That's not what you said.'

'My thoughts are wrestling. Fear versus fantasy.' She shifted, facing him, kneeling beside him, keeping hold of him, her naked thigh pressing against his. 'I told you my fear first, but I'm rooting for you being in Zach's life. I am. It's not that simple in my head. I'm scared, Ethan. It's all happening so fast.'

For a dozen heartbeats, he held still. Then his face moved fractionally toward her, gaze still downcast. 'Why are you scared?'

She couldn't say it. But their lives would suffer if it festered unspoken, so she whispered, 'You'll take him away from me.' Against her will, the tears returned, clogging her words. Ethan's hand covered hers, grip tight as he turned into her, frowning. 'The bond we have. I'm scared he'll grow to love you, and I'll lose a part of what I have with him. I've worked so hard to be everything he needs—and everything I want to be for him.' His shelter, his teacher, his mentor. Sparring partner, confidante, playmate. 'We're like a jigsaw puzzle, you know, and I've put us together exactly how I want, how he wants, and now I'm scared he'll give you the best pieces.'

Ethan didn't comment. Face lowered, his thumb stroked the back of her hand, and Stevie wondered if the anguish on his face also clung tight in his throat.

'I hate this feeling.' The urge to defend her riches from a man who had none. 'Another part of me is elated that you two are together.' A shaky inhale fractured her words. 'Genuinely, fiercely elated.'

'I know.' A broken mumble.

'It's just—he's my second heart.'

He looked up in awed sorrow. It took a few longs moments before he said, 'Do you want me to let you both leave? Let this be the end of it? I could do the birthday-card thing.'

She shook her head, distressed. 'No.'

Relief rode out on his sharp exhale. 'Then can we agree on an honesty system? When you feel something is changing, or fear that something is about to, you tell me. I can't help if I don't know. The last thing I want is to take over something you two have always done together.'

She and Zach had always done everything together.

She nodded anyway.

'That's not what this is about for me,' he said gently. 'I don't want to take pieces of your relationship with Zach. I want to build my own puzzle. But I'll need your help to figure out where the hell to start.'

His own puzzle. Did she feature in that future tableau? The three of them camping together. Standing with a teenage Zach between them at his graduation. Sitting down to dinner together as a family. Or was she out of the picture, unseen as she waited at home for Ethan to drop Zach off, waving from the apartment balcony as he drove away, not sure whether he ever looked up to see her?

'Things won't stay the same,' Ethan continued. 'But I'll try to make the changes good ones. For instance.' He paused, and his hold on her loosened. 'Pretend Zach doesn't exist.'

Stunned, she shot him a look of wet fury.

'Okay, bad choice of words.' Wincing, he raised a palm in apology. 'But we need to solve *our* problem now, because you can't make love like that and claim we're not going to work out. Don't shake your head—that's exactly my point.

Tell me what you'd want from me, if you didn't have to worry about Zach.'

'I'll always worry about Zach.'

'I know, Stevie.' Not exasperated, but reassuring. 'But I want to know if there's another reason—a non-Zach related reason—you don't want to be with me.'

Reluctantly, Stevie acknowledged the logic in his questioning. 'I would want you in my life.' The truth came out raw. 'My heart. My bed. I would do everything I could to impress you and make you want to spend your life with me.'

'I already want that.' He turned, palm pressing into the mattress on her other side, bringing himself against her. Confronted by the intensity of his powerful body, Stevie's resistance waned, and she surrendered, relaxing back onto the bed. He lay above her, hips sliding between her thighs, the promise of the position shooting heat right to her core.

She spoke against his mouth, body alight. 'But Zach does exist.'

His lips closed over hers for a sweet heartbeat before he propped up on one elbow and snuck his other palm down to span her thigh. 'And that means we can't?'

She ached for a future where she featured in their puzzle. 'There's too much in the way.'

'Give me the breakdown.'

Desire was stirring inside her. Instinctively, she shifted beneath him, body tingling, and Ethan used his hold to angle her leg to the side, opening her to him. The stirring kicked up into a forceful churn at the feel of his erection against her inner thigh, heavy, smooth. Voice catching, she answered, 'Zach wouldn't accept it. And pretending he did, you and I haven't actually spent time together. Lust isn't compatibility. We can't know that we'd even work.'

Compatible or not, this chemistry would last them a lifetime.

Ethan's fingers circled her knee. 'When do you go back to Melbourne?'

She shivered, arching beneath him. 'Two weeks.'

'I leave in a week and a half.' He paused. 'In that time, let's find out whether we're compatible.'

'But Zach—'

'Has the program to finish, and we have the painting. There's time to make this an informed decision.' His hand drifted up to the juncture of her thighs. There, his thumb traced lazy, seductive circles. 'This conversation isn't over. Say okay if you agree.'

Pleasure gathered beneath his touch, instantly impatient. 'Okay.'

'I'll take you out for lunch tomorrow. And every day after that.' His mouth closed over hers as he pushed inside her.

His kiss broke, and her pleasure soared. 'Okay.'

He inched down her body, all the better to reach her, resting one hand against her cheek. She gripped it, sighing, keeping him close. 'We'll make up for lost time. No questions are off-limits.'

'Okay.' The word scraped out on a rough exhale. Beautiful man with his languid touch and kisses against her stomach, luring her budding tension into bloom and holding it there as sensation rushed swiftly and sweetly to meet her.

'We'll make love every chance we get.'

Stevie peaked on a strangled breath, his strokes sure and slow, thumb still circling. She was moving beneath him, all of her, overcome as he let her ride it out, every tremor and pulse and prayer for this man's touch until the end of her days.

After, he gathered her against him, and she sank into his warmth, thinking she could rest just for a little while, her breathing growing even and her body weighing heavy into the mattress.

'Stevie,' he murmured into her hair. 'The last one.'

On her last breath before sleep, she whispered, 'Okay.'

THAT AFTERNOON, ZACH showed Ethan his rollerblading skills at the skate park. As Stevie stood beside her new lover in the setting sun, not touching, not talking, but occasionally meeting eyes in heated awareness, she felt something shifting at the very base of her existence. It wasn't until late that night, after she and Zach had watched the New Year's fireworks and he'd collapsed into bed, that she was able to translate the sensation into conscious thought.

She sat cross-legged on her bed, watching him sleep. Lying like a pin on his stomach, his face was turned toward her bed, his features at peace. His breaths came lightly, scarcely expanding his chest, his body sustained by the least air needed and taking no more than that.

Chin in her palm, Stevie couldn't deny that their lives were similar.

She and Zach shared a space—physical, emotional—the two of them together, with Felix nearby. An intimate existence, so very special, and she'd previously believed it needed to be protected at all costs. She hadn't considered that such exclusivity meant living on the bare minimum of human relationships.

Now Regan was back. Her runaway sister seeking a place by Stevie's side, and with no hard decisions there, three had suddenly become four. Disaster hadn't struck. Zach hadn't stopped loving his mother because he now had an aunt. He simply had another person to love.

Their lives, like Zach's sleeping lungs, had so much more space. If she could learn to breathe deeper, they could make room for Ethan, too. And they could both love him, without loving each other any less.

Things were starting to change.

And now, Stevie knew she wanted them to.

Chapter Ten

TIME PASSED TOO fast for Ethan. He'd been tricked by time before. Lost entire days, weekends, to ideas that sucked him in and only spat him out when his body's cries for food, light, and movement turned to neglected screams.

This was different.

He was aware of every second, felt the time rushing past like water beneath his surfboard—thrilling, fast, and no matter how he dragged his fingers through it, seeking a hold, it was ultimately intangible. He didn't want his time with Stevie and Zach to end, but he was powerless to stop it.

A mini routine formed. Zach went to the holiday program, and Ethan and Stevie painted together. In the late afternoons, he'd hang out with Stevie and Zach. When it came time to leave, he'd ask 'Same time tomorrow?' as casually as he could manage and hold his breath until Zach answered.

Sometimes, it was a close call, but ultimately, always a yes.

Zach's interest in Ethan waxed and waned. He'd be super keen to go surfing or boarding one afternoon, and then reticent the next, casting him closed-faced glances and hardly saying a word as they sat people watching at the wooden tables outside Lullabar. Stevie explained that some days he was able to live in the moment. Others, he was overwhelmed by the significance of Ethan's existence and hid behind silence.

On the final day of Zach's holiday program, just days before Ethan would move to Sydney, he once again took Stevie to lunch. They sat back from the bustle of the town in the quaint grounds of a wholefoods café, waiting for their meals beneath a large umbrella and pressing their bare feet into the cool grass.

'Ethan.' A black cap covered Stevie's pale hair, darkening the brown of her eyes to black as she watched him. Her shirt was grey, loose. He'd been beneath it once today, and he prayed to again before the afternoon was out. 'About your unique brand of brain…'

He stilled. An origami tutorial sat open on his phone browser—the peacock napkin was taking shape. He hadn't noticed himself become absorbed in the activity, but the folded swan and elephant on Stevie's placemat betrayed him. That possibly meant he'd tuned out in the middle of a conversation. His leg had almost certainly been jittering.

He slanted a glance at her. 'Sorry.'

'What for?'

Being weird. 'Do I embarrass you?'

'In front of all these people I don't know and will never

see again?' Her smile was wry. 'No.'

'In front of people you do know?' It hadn't escaped him that in all the hours they'd spent together, very few had been shared with Felix and her sister.

Lines formed on her brow. 'No. Of course not.'

He paused. 'What was your question?'

'I was curious about how it affects your work.'

Eyes flicking back to the next step on his screen, Ethan thought about it. 'I work odd hours,' he said, his hands resuming folding. 'Days where I do nothing but a few calls or emails are balanced out by days where I hardly leave the chair.' He flipped the napkin, creased a line. 'I forgot a lot of things in the early days, and I initially solved that with reminder alerts. But they were too easy to ignore, or forget to set up in the first place, so I invested in an assistant. He did all the admin and bookings for Let Us Bin It, and he figured out I needed him to be my memory, too. He moved businesses with me. The position plaque on his desk says, *Ethan's Puppeteer*. He's the only reason I seem outwardly competent as a CEO.'

He leaned back, recalling a particularly sterling example of how his head affected his work. 'I once missed a meeting because I got distracted counting and cooking spaghetti noodles, trying to determine exactly how many made an ideal single serve. I'm pretty sure that would only happen to someone of my kind of crazy.'

Stevie leaned forward, arms folded on the tabletop. He

prepared for a half-joking question about his supposed status as a functioning adult. But then, she asked, 'How many?'

Surprised, he breathed out a laugh. 'One hundred and forty-five for a chunky sauce. More like one hundred and seventy-five for a pesto.'

'That's highly valuable information.' Her gaze was warm, and her toes brushed his ankle under the table. 'Worth missing a meeting.'

Something precious unfurled in him, a moment before it was cast in shadow. 'I have a question for you,' he murmured.

Her glance was curious as she topped up her ice water.

'I shouldn't ask.' But the question had haunted him since she'd first stood on his doorstep.

As she lowered the pitcher, her shoulders set. Bracing herself, and rightly so.

'If you thought I'd died,' he said quietly, hands motionless now. 'Why didn't you go to my funeral?'

She sank beneath the question. Gaze down to her lap and shoulders curving in. It was a long half-minute before she answered. 'I agonized over it. I almost went. I thought seeing off the father of my baby would be the respectful thing to do. But then I realized I hadn't shown you any respect while you'd been alive. Attending would essentially be to make me feel better about myself—so I could reassure myself that in the end, I'd done right by you.' Her hands tangled on her thighs. Her toes dug into the grass, knuckles straining. 'How detestable to go to your funeral, when I didn't go to you while you were alive and tell you about Zach. How spineless to attend as if I'd known you, cared about you, when in reality, I'd avoided you and concealed the existence of your child.' She looked at him, mouth pinched, dark eyes anguished. 'I didn't deserve to go—to dilute the sorrow of those who knew and loved you, by selfishly seeking absolution.'

The subdued hum of street traffic was the only sound for several long moments.

'Stevie,' Ethan murmured, reaching for her. His fingers linked between hers. 'You've carried a lot of guilt.'

She didn't deny it.

'I thought you'd let it go the other day, when I told you I don't resent you. But you haven't.'

She didn't deny that either. Her eyes were still set on her lap.

'I want you to stop now.'

Her head shook before she caught herself.

His thumb brushed over her knuckles. 'You drop your guilt, and I'll drop mine at having caused yours.'

The struggle was live on her face as she looked up. 'That's not fair.'

'Imagine my guilt as a barge that has to accommodate for the size of yours. No matter what, mine will always be bigger.'

'Ethan...'

'We're living now, Stevie. Drop the past.'

He waited, watched, and slowly, so slowly, the lines of struggle on her brow eased, replaced by wariness. Like perhaps she wasn't sure how to feel without such a burden.

'And don't even think about feeling guilty about not feeling guilty,' he said, pointing at her.

Wry amusement twisted her lips. 'Fine. I promise.'

'Good.' He smiled gently. 'I'd like to hang out with Felix and Regan.'

She blinked at his topic shift. 'Okay.'

'If I don't embarrass you.'

'I'll talk to them,' she said, kicking him under the table. 'We'll all hang out.'

'SO, I WAS thinking maybe I could visit you back home sometime.'

Ethan's words sounded surprisingly whole considering they had to pass around the heart in his throat. He, Zach, and Stevie sat on the beach, fish-and-chip paper crumpled and empty on the sand. Seagulls clustered around them, squawking and fighting, venturing close before racing away, wings flapping in a fluster. The sun was lowering behind them, and the warm sea breeze brushed past their bare shoulders. Zach had been wiping a finger through the batter crumbs and salt, waving off the birds as he consumed every last greasy fleck.

Now, he grew still. The glance he shot at Ethan held uncertainty.

'Don't have to decide now.' Ethan assumed an easy posture, leaning back on his palms. 'I was just putting it out there—that I'm interested if you are.'

His eyes met Stevie's over Zach's head. She looked as on edge as he felt.

'Like,' Zach said, turning away from the paper to run his hands through the sand. 'What would we do?'

Hang out—eat—skate—shit, what else—bowl—golf—not their style—fish—hadn't fished a day in his life—they could camp—get Stevie's okay—hike—do charity runs—or whatever Zach wanted—shouldn't presume—could be interested in the stage—kitchen—fashion—patternmaking—Ethan could get behind that—he had clothing ideas—father-son business— international clothing label—oh, he needed a new shirt—shop online—ask Daniel—and to set up a call with Disrupt Global—damn, what was the question?

'Hmm?' he said, scrabbling backwards.

'What would you do?' Stevie murmured.

'Whatever you want, Zach.'

Zach didn't answer as he dragged sand together, the beginnings of a structure.

'We could go out or stay home,' Ethan said.

More sand, more silence.

'For as long or as little as you want.' He shared another look with Stevie. She gave a tiny nod, encouraging, so he kept talking. 'Ten minutes or all afternoon.'

A double handful of sand landed smack on top of the low mound.

'Up to you,' he finished, resisting the urge to run a hand over his eyes.

Zach kept looking down; kept piling sand.

'Maybe,' Zach said, finally, in an uncharacteristic mumble. 'Maybe I could show you my books.'

Deep within, Ethan glowed, convinced those few words had just granted him a longer life. He was going to buy Zach a book—a whole series—the next chance he got. 'I'd like that.' He made himself pause. 'You probably want a break from having to see me, though. We could leave it until you're back at school.'

'Nah, come sooner.' Zach looked up, stunning Ethan with his own eyes. He'd never get used to that. Zach's shoulder rose, a shrug to accompany his confession. 'I like hanging out.'

Stevie turned her face away, hand covering her mouth.

'All right.' This time, the heart-shaped hole in his words made them breathy and broken.

Zach resumed building what appeared to be a sand circus tent. 'Ethan?'

A curious grunt was all he could safely manage.

'Could you bring Hack?'

THE YOGA RETREAT was a twenty-minute drive out of town,

secreted away in the hinterland. Sheltered by trees in the heart of the blue-green mountains, the building was so quiet, so at peace, that Stevie caught herself holding her breath as she waited in the entrance hall. The walls didn't quite deserve such a name, as they were more open space than timber, possibly allowing for an internal-external energy flow or some kind of outside-while-inside experience. She tried to let the soft music and essential oils have the desired effect, but she was too full of conviction that this was a stupid idea to have space for calm.

'It's not stupid.' Regan stood beside her, gazing outward. 'It's practical.'

'I feel like an arsehole.'

She felt more than saw her sister's frown. 'Everyone does it.'

'Everyone goes behind their lover's back to corner his best friend in order to learn private details about said lover?'

Regan paused. 'Okay, so I'm not the best representative of normal social behavior. Stepping down.'

Stevie eyed her dryly. 'What question should I start with?'

'How about that one on whether his ADHD means you and Zach might not hold his attention for long?'

Grimacing, she said, 'I might ease into that one.'

No sound came from behind them, but they both became simultaneously aware of a new presence in the room. Turning together, they found Vikas approaching on bare feet. Unassuming and silent—an eavesdropper's ideal skillset.

'Stevie,' he greeted, glancing curiously at her younger sister. 'And…'

'Regan,' Stevie introduced. The pair nodded at each other, smiles polite, before Vikas gestured toward the kartini chairs near one of the open walls. The wood was carved in a graceful arc, maintaining the general delicacy of the retreat. Billowy curtains, finely colored paintings, and intricately engraved furniture. Even the nearby gumtrees had long, elegant leaves that dripped like silver from the branches. Stevie's bulky shorts and black T-shirt seemed abrasive in contrast, and she sat a little straighter, tucking her feet away under the seat, knees and heels together.

'Sorry to interrupt you at work,' she said, keeping her voice low despite their isolation. The receptionist who had sought Vikas had not returned to the greeting desk.

'Not at all.' He smiled. 'How's Zach?'

'Good.' Playing computer games with Felix. 'He's having an inside day. Your program wiped him out.'

His smile grew. 'That's what I like to hear. Now, would you prefer to ease into that question, or shall I just answer?'

'Oops,' Regan murmured, turning toward Stevie in apology.

With another grimace, she said, 'Maybe just answer.'

'You're worried he's only interested in you two because you're new and shiny?'

There was that arsehole feeling. 'Kind of.'

'That's not how he works.'

Stevie's lungs emptied in relief.

'He doesn't get bored of things that matter to him. But he can get restless if he doesn't have enough things that matter. So,' he said, tilting his head. 'He's not cut out for a lifestyle of quiet nights in front of the television, regardless of how much he loves you.'

Stevie nodded. That suited her fine.

'I've researched it.' Vikas watched a kookaburra as it swooped past. 'Initially as an instructor, then as a friend. I'm not going to lie. It's complicated, and—as he refuses to forget—not strictly conducive to relationships.'

'A lot of things aren't conducive to relationships.' Regan sat with one leg crossed over the other, her flip-flop tapping lightly against her moving foot. 'But we make them work.'

'Yes.' Impassive, Vikas turned to Stevie. 'You're here to work out whether or not to pursue him?'

'I'm here for you to tell me what I need to know in order to pursue him.'

His mask of composure cracked beneath a delighted grin.

'He calls himself a nutcase,' she said.

The grin faded. 'He says his mind is like playing the Wikipedia game. Starts with one thought, then clicks through to another, and another, and within ten seconds, he's thinking about something entirely different and can't necessarily remember where he started.'

She had noticed that.

'You get used to it.' Vikas sat still, shoulders down, back straight. 'He'd probably hate it, but in conversational terms, I think of him as a stray thread. A part of the weave, *wanting* to be a part of the weave, but sometimes, he tugs loose and needs to be picked up and subtly threaded back into place.'

'He would hate that,' she agreed. Hate that he caused others the effort of drawing him back.

'He can't see the good in the way he is.'

Stevie resolved to make it happen.

Over the next half an hour, Vikas masterfully fulfilled his best-friend role by convincing them of Ethan's decency and value. Not that Stevie had doubted his worth, not this time around. As the sisters walked toward the exit, Regan murmured, 'I'll watch TV with you. Movie marathons, boxset binges, whatever you need.'

Stevie grinned. 'Thanks, Reegs.'

'Stevie.' Vikas spoke from behind them, and she turned, brows raised. 'Just remember that it affects his head, not his heart.'

She almost laughed.

That, right there, was everything she needed to hear.

STEVIE SEEMED DIFFERENT. Since she and Zach had met Ethan on the beach, she wouldn't quite meet his stare. Her gaze kept slipping away, denying him access to the emotion in her eyes. Zach had spent the day shooting 'em up, so they washed the glaze from his face with a swim, and then Ethan and Stevie sat high up on the sand, while Zach played in the sand near the water.

Ethan leaned back on his palms. Vik had called him earlier. Apparently, Stevie had paid him a visit. Wouldn't tell him why, and he made Ethan promise not to reveal that he knew.

Ethan desperately wanted to know why.

'Stop staring at me,' she murmured, rubbing sunscreen over her shins.

'Have you dated?' he asked, and he was rewarded when her gaze clashed into his, startled.

'Uh. Not really.' She tugged at the brim of her cap, stare shifting to Zach. A ghost of a smile moved at the corners of her mouth. 'The closest I've come is a few one-nighters with guys I met at soccer.'

'You and I have been together more than one night.'

The ghost vanished. He received one of those slippery glances. 'Yeah.'

'So.' He left it at that.

'So, yes, you're the closest I've come to dating. But Zach is still in the dark, which means this whole thing is a bit terrifying, and I'm trying not to panic.'

It took every ounce of self-control for Ethan not to demand specifics on *this whole thing.*

'Have you had many girlfriends?' she asked, voice tight.

He raked his fingers though the sand. 'I guess.'

'Tell me about them.'

'They were nice,' he said, thinking back over the years. 'I enjoyed their company, but they weren't necessarily prepared for mine. Not their fault.'

Stevie twisted to face him, features in shadow. 'It always ended because of you?'

'Nutcase,' he reminded her.

'Stop that.' Her frown was serious as she pointed at him. 'We need a different word.'

'Crazy. Screwy. Deficient.'

That propelled the finger into his side, digging in. 'You do *not* have an attention deficit,' she said firmly. 'You're attention different. Curse whoever named ADHD, for implying it's a bad thing.' Eyes narrowed, she glared at passersby. 'God, I hate language. Nothing should have that much power over us.'

And God, Ethan adored Stevie. He embraced the power she had over him, just by being her. The power to surprise him, humble him, and delight him.

And this—the power to make him suspect he'd been placed in a mislabeled box his whole life.

'I mean, the word tomboy,' she went on. Her finger still dug into his ribs, but Ethan didn't care. 'Honestly. Boys don't own the qualities that make a girl a tomboy. Are those girls supposed to think that their own gender is so inferior that they want to dis-identify with being a girl entirely? What the hell?'

Captivated, he didn't answer.

'And Tom is a boy's name. So essentially, we're double male. It could at least be a tomgirl, or, I don't know, polly-boy or something. But even that's placing certain qualities into the boy box, when I'm clearly a girl, and so liking sport and science are therefore unisex qualities. Tomboy shouldn't even exist as a term.'

Ethan collected her hand from his side. Stroking his thumb over her knuckles, he said, 'I love your brain.'

She spun to face him, brows still lowered. 'And I love yours. Never believe otherwise.'

He almost dropped her hand.

No one had ever said that to him before.

Slowly, he watched her own statement sink in. She blinked, blushed, and then awkwardly retrieved her hand.

'Like I said,' she muttered, attention fixing on Zach down the shore. 'There's a lot of power in words.'

ON THE DAY before Ethan's flight, Stevie came good on her promise to hang out with Felix and Regan. Ethan brought Hack down to the beach, Regan borrowed a net and ball from the Lullabar storeroom, and Zach dictated that he should get an extra person on his team because he was only little.

'What are you talking about?' Stevie kicked him lightly in the bum as she moved to help set the net up. 'You're the extra person.'

Ethan swallowed a laugh from where he secured a pole into the sand.

'That's it!' Zach waved an arm melodramatically. 'Mum's not on my team.'

Grinning, Stevie briefly met Ethan's eye from the opposite pole. His stomach flipped, and his smile broke through. 'Who's on your team, then?' she asked.

'Felix. And Ethan.'

'Battle of the sexes.' Regan was gathering the fabric of her T-shirt around her waist, forming two ends and tying them together. 'Fascinating.'

Zach marched over as Felix and Ethan gathered on one side of the net. Stopping between the men, he spat, 'Darn it.'

'Regret?' Ethan murmured down at his blond head.

'Always be on Stevie's team,' Felix said, tossing the ball from hand to hand.

'She's good at volleyball?'

'She's good at everything.'

Zach crossed his arms, facing his mother. 'I've made a huge mistake.'

True enough, the women thrashed them.

Had he tended toward emasculation, Ethan could have placated his pride and soothed his loss with the fact that he hadn't slept properly in days. Not with anxiety rubbing him raw like coarse grit sandpaper. If he'd once thought to distract himself from the ache in his ribcage, the pressure of impending loss, his time with Stevie and Zach had amplified it tenfold. Not only was he leaving Byron Bay behind, with its surf-perfect beaches and Vikas's steady presence, but he was also parting ways with the woman of his dreams and the son he yearned to love.

The promise of visiting Zach was no small relief, but Stevie had yet to confirm what she saw happening between them, and their time was almost up.

'Going to congratulate the winner?' Stevie had moved to his side of the net, smile victorious. Her hand hung high, waiting for a high five.

Meeting her palm with his, Ethan then swiftly laced his fingers through hers and pulled her hand down between them. 'Congratulations,' he murmured, letting go before Zach could see. 'I say we're compatible. Can we talk later?'

Startled, she darted a look over her shoulder to where Zach was busy trying to poke Regan in the stomach. 'Uh, yeah.'

'Before my farewell party.'

'Isn't that a surprise?'

'Theoretically.'

She frowned. 'I'll ask Felix to mind Zach for a bit.'

Too preoccupied by what she might say, Ethan opted out of the next game. He sat beside Hack, rubbing between the dog's brows. Felix joined them, drinking from a water bottle and running a hand across his forehead. Regan and Stevie had split, playing each other, and unsurprisingly, Zach had joined his mother's team.

Both men sat silent, watching the game.

Finally, the opportunity became too much. Ethan cleared his throat. 'I know it'd be wrong to thank you for looking out for them all these years.'

Felix's answer was tight. 'You'd be right.'

'But it sickens me to think of how she would've struggled without you, because Zach's screw-up father wasn't fit to help.' A look at Felix showed him rigid: feet planted in the sand with his knees raised, hands behind him. 'I know you didn't do it for me. But thanks.'

Felix's jaw slid. Then he shot a sideways glance at Ethan. 'Don't thank me.'

Ethan cocked a brow.

'I only asked Stevie to move out with me because Regan made me promise before she ran away. It was—complicated.'

'You'd have done it anyway, when you found out.'

Felix didn't deny it, but he continued, 'I supported her decision not to track you down. I told her not to go to your—your brother's—funeral. It was killing her. I said it wouldn't change anything, except make her feel worse with the postnatal depression and everything.' Felix slid off his glasses and pressed a hand to the bridge of his nose. Dismayed at this new piece of information, Ethan watched Stevie pass the ball to Zach, who hit it directly into the net. 'If I'd just let her go, none of this would have happened.'

Ethan held down a groan. 'No, it wouldn't have. Things

would have been much worse. Look,' he said. 'I've done this guilt thing with Stevie already. Mind if you just get over it so we can both move on?'

Felix looked startled.

'No, I don't care.' He raised his palms. 'I care that it's more my fault than yours.'

Taken aback, the other man looked him in the eye. 'You'll be good for her. She needs someone like you.'

Ethan inclined his head, but he said, 'I don't think she *needs* anyone.'

'That's the problem.' Stevie's friend shook his head. 'She's convinced every one of that, including herself.'

Frowning, Ethan watched Stevie ace the ball, landing on her knees in the sand with her arms raised in triumph. Cheering, Zach leapt onto her back, and she pushed to her feet, running around with his arm locked around her neck. She was strong. She was competent. She was in control.

Felix was right.

Watching, Ethan realized the danger with Stevie's strong bearings. The easy assumption was that she was capable, coping fine on her own, no help needed. But strength was one step away from stoicism, and that could disguise all manner of woe where help was desperately needed, but untrained at being sought.

'She'd convinced me,' he said, quiet.

'I'll never stop being in awe of her.' Felix held up an arm, deflecting sand spray as Stevie and Zach ran past. 'But I do think you'll be good for her.'

'It kind of sounds like you're giving me your blessing.'

Felix shifted, uncomfortable. 'There's nothing she can't handle. Won't handle. But don't make the mistake of assuming it's easy for her to do it. Take advantage of her strength, and I'll be tapping you on the shoulder.'

Ethan eyed him, serious. 'Sounds fair.'

Felix drank from his water bottle again. 'May I question one minor detail, in what I assume is a plan to live happily ever after?'

'Sure.'

'What does Zach think?'

Chapter Eleven

S TEVIE WENT HOME with Ethan under the pretense of helping him with last-minute packing, and under the double pretense of keeping him away from Lullabar until the farewell party had been set up.

The real reason had Ethan pressing her against the door the instant it closed behind them, hands sliding under her loose shirt and peeling it over her head in one swift movement.

'These shirts,' he murmured, mouth moving to her neck, 'are the best.'

'Ethan,' she breathed, arousal swiftly taking hold. As always, its grip was tight-fisted and undeniable, and her body bent beneath his touch, impatient as ever. 'We were going to talk.'

But no, apparently she'd missed this part of the plan, because there was no talking, just breathing, and touching, and kissing. Kisses that devoured her strength and flared the love in her heart as her clothes dropped and his followed, and then she was melting at the feel of his skin, and groaning at the pause it took to tug a packet from his wallet, and aching as he lifted her to his waist and pressed himself hard and naked between her thighs as she slid over him during their deepest kiss yet.

Thirty seconds in the door, and he was moving inside her.

Stevie's body throbbed, inflamed by his rhythm. This intensity still stunned her. The need that reached for him every moment he wasn't touching her; the ache that haunted her when he wasn't around, scaring off appetite, concentration, peace.

'Stevie.' It sounded like a prayer. His movements were slick and growing faster. Clutching him, she watched his face flicker with the fear that this might be it. The last time. That maybe, despite chemistry, despite fate throwing them this curveball of a second chance, they wouldn't be able to make it work, and this would become nothing but a crazy, totally messed-up affair.

No, she couldn't let this go.

She couldn't hide it.

She had one choice.

'I'll tell him,' she whispered, whimpered, as urgency opened wide and swallowed her whole. Bliss was delivered with the impact of a hot punch, made sweeter by the sound and sensation of Ethan finding his own release.

Ethan was worth the risk.

When he lifted his face from her neck, holding her steady, he asked, 'You sure?'

'Yes.'

His gaze searched her face. 'You think we could work?'

'I want to find out,' she said, and he grinned with such undiluted delight that her heart felt his light. 'I want to be with you,' she said, certainty strong in her words. 'Hold your hand. Go on date nights. Let you sleep in my bed.' Excitement flipped in her stomach at the thought of a life with Ethan. Taking it slow, sharing days here and nights there, until they just so happened to share every day and night, unable to live apart. Her lover, Zach's father.

Zach. Her excitement fled, chased by apprehension. 'But Zach has to be okay with it.'

'What will you say to him?'

She raised a shoulder, breath still unsteady. 'I don't know.' This trip had been a series of incredibly difficult conversations. One more and life had to cut her a break, surely? 'I'll just...be honest.'

Ethan's response was slow, features guarded. 'Will he be okay with it?'

Prediction churned inside her. He'd never been okay with her dating in the past. But this was different. She needed this so badly that she couldn't fathom an alternative. 'I hope so,' she said, not really answering the question.

Hope dared to flicker in his eyes. 'We're really going to try this?'

The flip returned to her belly. 'Yes?'

'Such certainty.' The blade of his nose swiped hers.

'I want it to work.' She wanted it so badly. 'But Zach aside, Ethan, it's still a mess. I've been trying to think of a solution for days, but I keep coming up blank.'

He frowned, etching lines between his brows.

'You're moving to Sydney, remember?' Distractedly, she pressed a quick kiss to his forehead to smooth the lines. His body stiffened against her, gaze ardent. 'Your community project is important to so many people, including you.' Giving up such a positive social and environmental impact wasn't an option. 'And we can't leave Melbourne. Zach's school and friends are there. He's settled, and we have Felix nearby. And now Regan—she's going to move in with him. I haven't spent time with my sister since we were teenagers, so I can't move to Sydney, I just—'

'Hey.' Ethan eased her feet to the floor, standing back. 'Little problems. All just little problems.'

She stared. They really weren't.

'Leave it with me,' he said, fingers trailing down her arm. Then he smiled so genuinely that, in that moment, she believed he could think them out of this impossible corner. 'You talk to Zach. I'll figure out the other stuff.'

Zach.

Anxiety scrunched inside her.

'Meet at your farewell party?' She managed a faint smile. 'Pretend we planned to meet there for dinner or something, as a part of my sneaky scheme to get you to Lullabar?'

'Okay.' He gathered their clothes, lines reforming between his brows. Distractedly, he folded her shirt and shorts before passing them over.

Taking them with an amused brow raise, she added, 'Vikas said six-thirty.'

'Six-thirty.' He sounded preoccupied as he tugged on his shorts.

'That's in an hour.'

Ethan straightened, looking into the middle distance as he dutifully repeated, 'An hour.'

WHEN STEVIE RETURNED, the back section of Lullabar had been roped off to the general public. Vikas was talking with Parker beside the rope, holding the hand of a toddler struggling to reach the snack bowls and platters on the cordoned-off booths. A sign hung partway up the high wall, silver letters reading *Good Luck, Ethan!* The words glinted and curled under the gust of the fans, and their generic cheer, their fleeting significance, brought her to a sudden halt.

Ethan always moved on.

How many farewell parties had been thrown in his honor? How many plastic banners had been jammed in the rubbish, no longer needed as his taillights flickered goodbye the next morning? How many times had he not wanted to leave, not really, but believed he had no choice because he feared the consequences of his overactive mind?

Stevie stared at the sign, pulse lurching.

He believed in a life with her and Zach.

Ethan wasn't the type to bask in overconfidence. He wouldn't believe their relationship would work out simply because he wanted it to. After an adulthood of moving, he must know, somehow, that he would stay.

The magnitude of that had her taking the stairs three at a time. Felix and Regan had their hotel room door open, both sprawled on the bed reading, and told her that Zach had wanted to read on his own bed instead—the open door was to ensure he didn't try to sneak off again. But true to his wishes, Stevie found Zach lying on his bed with his phone up in his face. One leg hung off the side of the mattress, and the other heel was propped up on her bed, a tidy pile of sand around it. Closing the door, Stevie sat down opposite him, nudging his foot and brushing off the sand, feigning ease while trying to remember to breathe.

Please, Zach, her heart begged. *Please let me have this.*

'What are you doing?' she asked, easy to start.

He didn't look up. 'Reading Jed's comic.'

Stevie frowned. 'Not the one with ghosts?'

Zach eyes darted across his screen. 'There's a twist, Mum. It's amazing.'

The twist was in her chest, getting tighter and tighter. She ran her hand over his knee and shook him a little. 'I want to talk to you about something.'

'Because like the whole time, he's helping ghosts with their unfinished business, but doesn't talk to any live people, because he's homeless and doesn't know anyone.' His attention continued to track across the screen. 'And *now,* we've just found out there was an apocalypse, and he's the only person who survived. And he's just realized that even if he helps ghosts for the rest of his life, he won't be able to help them all, 'cause it's like, all of Earth, and when he dies, that'll be his unfinished business, but there won't be anyone left alive to help *him.*'

'So he's doomed to haunt a dead planet for all eternity?' Stevie plucked the phone from his grip. 'That's messed up. You shouldn't be reading that.'

He looked smug. 'I'm basically finished anyway.'

Putting it behind her, she rallied her strength. 'I want to talk to you about Ethan.'

'Yeah?' He sat up, earnest. 'When can he visit? Because I thought we could go watch the next Marvel film.'

That jerked her off track. 'But you and I always watch them together.'

His eyes rolled. 'I meant all of us, Mum.'

'Oh. Cool.' Inhaling, Stevie tried to mimic Vikas— shoulders down, spine straight. But calm eluded her. 'About Ethan,' she repeated, fingers knotting on her lap. 'I wanted to ask you something. It's important.'

He shuffled up the bed, resting against his pillow. 'What?'

'He and I have been hanging out a lot, with the painting, and spending time together with you.' Nerves tumbled in her stomach, prickly, itchy. 'We're getting on really well.'

He frowned, shrugging a shoulder. 'Good?'

'It is good. And I was hoping that while you and Ethan are continuing to hang out, getting to know each other, you wouldn't mind if Ethan and I did the same thing.'

His frown froze. 'Like, alone?'

She couldn't lie. Keeping her chin level, she answered, 'Maybe sometimes.'

The frown didn't budge. 'Doing what?'

'Getting to know each other.'

'Why?' His arms crossed again.

'Because I like him, Zach,' she said, struggling to keep her words easy. 'And people spend time with people they like.'

'What do you mean you *like him*?' he demanded, body stiffening on the soft bed.

He knew what she meant.

Reaching out, Stevie took his hand, reminding herself that she'd expected this reaction. She had to push through, help him to understand and accept it. 'I mean I like him. In the same way Felix and Regan like each other.'

'But they're in love.' He tried to tug his hand out of hers, but she held tight. 'They hold hands and kiss each other. You and Ethan don't do that. You only hang out because of me.'

Her silence had him sitting bolt upright, eyes wide. 'Mum,' he said, a fearful warning.

'This doesn't have to be a bad thing.' With her free hand, Stevie gripped the bedsheets by her side. 'You like Ethan. You know him.'

Panic was bright on his face. 'I like him for me, not for you.'

'Why not for both of us? You just said you wanted us to all see a film together.'

'It's a stupid movie, Mum.' Tears gathered in his eyes, dampening her hope. 'This isn't what I meant!'

'Don't yell at me.' Alarm struck up a beat beneath her collarbones. 'I want you to think about this.'

'I have! You told me it was my choice.' He yanked suddenly and broke out of her grip, scrabbling away from her off the bed. 'And I don't want you and Ethan to be a thing. That's my choice!'

'Don't I get to help choose?' Her hand lowered, joining the other at clutching the sheet. It wouldn't help if she got worked up. She had to stay composed, sitting down.

He didn't answer. His back was turned, shoulders clenched and neck rigid.

'You'll always come first, Zach.' Her throat grew tight as he tried to open the door to the balcony, tried to escape from her, but she'd slid the top bolt in that morning, so he just stood there, cranking the handle and shaking the door. 'I love you more than anything.' Her words sounded strained, forced through pain. 'I always will.'

He gave up on the handle and pounded his fist on the

doorframe. His forehead followed. 'You can't,' he said bleakly.

At that, the truth lodged like ice in her chest.

Zach wasn't going to accept this.

'I want you to support me.' *Please, please give me this.* 'Can you do that?'

'Yes.' He spun around, face red. 'But Ethan can't! I'm going to support you with your homework, but he just made you work on your holiday. That's not support!'

'He didn't make me.' Stevie stood up, body weak, but she granted him distance. 'He's a good guy; you know he is.'

'I don't care!' he shouted, hands balled by his sides.

'Please, Zach.' The begging in her heart was so fierce it forced its way to her mouth. 'Please. I want to spend time with him. Maybe sometimes you'll go to Felix's place, and I'll hang out with Ethan while you're there. I don't want to lie and pretend I'm alone. I want you to be okay with me and him being together.'

'Well, it's not okay!'

'I won't be taking away your time with him. You'll still get to—'

'I don't want to see him anymore!'

The blood drained from her skull, leaving her cold. She hadn't even considered that he'd reject Ethan entirely. 'That's not fair—'

'It is! I told him to leave us alone. And he didn't. I don't want to see him ever again!'

'Zach.' Stevie chased reason, desperate not to get worked up. But reason outran her, and her voice rose. 'He's not going to take me away from you. No one's getting replaced.'

'Exactly.' Not a winning argument, but the raw emotion he spat out with the word refused defeat. Then he said, 'Go away,' as he pressed his back against the balcony door, sliding down until he was sitting, face pressed against his knees.

Stevie tore, pain travelling outwards. Searing out from her heart, across her ribcage, as if this argument had just ripped Ethan from her life, her future, and she felt the loss as a physical wound.

'Zach.' He voice shook. 'We need to talk about—'

'I said *go away!*'

Pulse pounding, eyes flooding, Stevie felt the fight leave her. Never had she allowed him to win an argument before, but this wasn't about chores or homework. This was about her future. She managed to get the door open and shut behind her, before turning and almost colliding into Felix and Regan. Their stricken faces betrayed having overheard the shouting, and it took the last of her strength to keep her head high.

'I've ruined everything,' she whispered, trembling.

Regan swallowed, forcing a pitiful smile. 'He'll come around.'

Stevie ran a hand under her eyes, but the tears kept coming. 'No.' Her voice cracked. 'I stopped thinking clearly. I thought—thought…' She'd thought she could have it all. But her life had never worked like that. It had been foolish to think it would start now. 'And now Ethan will have nothing.'

Felix was shaking his head.

'It can't—I can't be selfish.' Her voice caught, and her tears spilled. 'It distresses him too much. It always has.' Zach's crying was muted through the door, but the sound still battered at her, amplifying her own distress. 'He comes first; he has to.'

Zach would always come first.

'This isn't right.' Distress was bright on Regan's face. 'You and Ethan make sense.'

'Maybe when he's older,' Stevie said in a small voice. 'Can you be with him? I can't right now.'

Her sister nodded, features falling.

'I'll go wait for Ethan.' And tell him that she'd destroyed his fragile relationship with Zach, and any hope that they could form a family. That no matter how compatible they were, this couldn't happen, because she had more than herself to consider. On leaden feet, Stevie moved down the hall. At the top of the stairs, she looked back, soul crying for reassurance that she would recover from this, and saw Regan opening the door, sending Zach's bawling into the corridor.

Felix was still shaking his head.

ETHAN HAD IT figured out. Not every detail, but in terms of the big picture, he could see how he and Stevie could make it work. It'd be unconventional, but that wouldn't be a new space for either of them, and if he were honest, attempts at normality had probably contributed to his past of failed relationships.

He jogged to meditate, for God's sake. He wasn't cut out for a lotus life.

He parked and strode toward the bar, the night air tropical, the sky black and sparkling overhead. He had no idea what time Stevie had said. Once he'd sat down to figure out their future, time had spun away from him, out of sight, out of mind, but knowing Vik's preference for early nights, Ethan was definitely late.

Inside, he hit the crowd immediately. A busy venue on most nights, he suspected the farewell event had the public patrons cramming into even tighter confines. Ethan maneuvered past men in board shorts, women in skirts and bikini tops, all pressing together to form one loud, laughing cluster of people. When he reached the back of the room, a sea of familiar faces all turned to look at him, breaking into relieved smiles and shouting, 'Surprise!'

Emotion gripped beneath his breastbone.

He hated farewell parties.

He hated leaving.

'Hey!' Ethan pretended disbelief. 'What's all this about?'

Vik disentangled himself from the gathering and clasped

him on the shoulder. 'Right on time,' he said, smiling. 'And I'm going to miss saying that.'

Ethan placed his hand over Vik's and squeezed. He was going to miss everything about this man. 'Pretty sure I said no party.'

'It's for the rest of us.'

In a long glance, Ethan noted various people who'd made up his life in Byron, casual friends, acquaintances, neighbors. He scanned for Stevie, looking into face after face, his pulse kicking up in unfounded alarm when he couldn't see her. She'd be here. He'd felt the truth hours earlier, as she'd clenched around him, drawing him deeper, finding the bliss in his body and hauling it into hers. She'd told him she wanted to hold his hand—to welcome him into her bed. Stevie wouldn't say something like that if she didn't mean it.

She'd be here.

Then guests started closing in, shaking his hand, giving him cards, and wishing him the best. He thanked them as graciously as he could manage with his attention elsewhere, distractedly darting around the room, seeking the one person who mattered most of all, the only woman he didn't intend to leave behind, not again, not ever.

As his personal trainer stepped back into the throng, he murmured to Vik, 'Stevie here?'

Oddly neutral, Vik inclined his head toward the booths.

One person shifted, another bent down, and there she was.

Sitting at the end of a booth, facing outwards, her knees together and hands locked in her lap. Contained, closed off, with her face downcast and shoulders rolled in. Regan sat next to her, watching Ethan without expression. At his look, her mouth moved, and she rested a hand on her sister's back.

Stevie looked up. Her dark gaze caught and dropped his in the same second. Then she was standing, winding her way toward him, inching herself between guests, all the while keeping her face down. His tension strung and Ethan frowned, sliding a hand into his pocket.

This was bad—what would he do—cope—run—beg—if she said no—Lord—give him strength—he'd dealt with a lot— grief—failure—but not darkness after pure light—wouldn't see again—wouldn't want to—stand straight—this was definitely bad—straighter—she was close—chin up—don't cry—don't run—just wait—wait to know for certain.

Just wait.

Noise shoved at him, music, laughter, shouting, and he wanted to drown it out, swipe it aside, give himself silence to deal with the love of his life approaching him with sadness in her step, but it pounded on, adding to the rising buzz in his head.

Stevie reached him.

He held his breath until his lungs burned.

'I'm sorry,' she murmured. Words that would have been quiet in a silent room, and were scarcely audible here. But Ethan heard.

Dread sickened him.

No. He hadn't actually believed—

'Maybe we should go outside?' she managed.

Stiff, he nodded.

The sky seemed darker as they were released from the crowd, the music, the general atmosphere of buoyancy. Out here, beyond the wooden tables, they could sink in solitude.

Jaw tight, Ethan faced her. 'Say it.'

'It's not going to work.' She spoke to the sand.

The pressure at the pit of his stomach grew—the crash site of a collapsing dream.

He was really leaving.

Without Stevie.

She'd spoken about lives being like jigsaw puzzles. In only weeks, she'd witnessed the impossible puzzle of his life—no straight edges and an indistinguishable final image—and had still somehow placed herself neatly against him, around him. He knew without a doubt he'd never meet someone who could interlock with his edgeless existence as perfectly as Stevie.

He groaned, raising a hand to his head.

'I'm sorry,' she whispered, staring at his chest, features lifeless. 'I wish things could be different.'

He waited, turning into her, her body beckoning like a heat source, but there was no warmth in her tonight, only the chill of her own dejection.

'Zach.' Her voice was heavy with apology. 'He's not okay with it.'

He ordered himself to stand straight, staying close as the coldness spread. 'Is it me?'

'It's anyone.'

Swallowing, Ethan ducked his face and nodded.

'He...' she said, and he watched her toes dig into the sand. 'He said he doesn't want to see you anymore, but I'll work on him, I promise. He came around once, and he will again. But we should give it a month or two before you visit him. He got pretty worked up. I'm really sorry.'

Ethan broke in so many places. Zach didn't want to see him. Zach didn't want him to see Stevie. And even though her son forbade her from having a partner, Stevie was going to do everything she could to give him a father, and Ethan a son. Selflessness didn't get any purer.

'He won't come around to the idea of us.' She was defeated, still staring at his chest. 'I've tried to date before, halfhearted attempts, but he doesn't change his mind. It distresses him. Maybe in a few years, or when he's older...'

Throat sore, soul weeping, Ethan nodded again.

'You'll find someone else.' Her words of reassurance only sharpened the pain. 'That's okay. I'll be happy for you.'

'I won't.'

At that, she finally looked up, wide eyes anguished. 'Please.'

Ethan shook his head. This wasn't right.

None of this was right.

'Be angry with me,' he said.

She tipped her head, frowning, helpless.

'It's always been easier when I've done something wrong. Caused it, somehow. I understand that; I can move on from that.' He couldn't move on from this.

'Ethan.' His name spoken quiet and tender. 'There's nothing wrong with you.'

His throat cramped. 'That's not helping.'

The only woman who had ever believed him perfect was going to turn her back on him. Then he realized. She was being stoic, submitting to the situation without complaint, despite her dreams caving in.

'At what point do you put yourself first?' He lowered his voice as a couple wandered past, feet in the shallows, a romantic stroll along the beach. He envied them their soft laughter, their enjoined fingers, when he would never hold Stevie again. 'Or at least stop putting yourself second? You need to be happy too, Stevie.'

For a long time, she stared at him. Then she shook her head and whispered, 'I have no idea.'

He heard the unspoken phrase at the end. *But not now.*

This was it—the end—he'd fly to Sydney—live alone—no visits—no relationship—no son—no perfect woman—him and Hack—always just him and Hack—no one to ask about his day—work—ideas—hundreds of ideas—he'd be lonely— missing her—every day—she was the quiet—the pleasure—the goal—the urgency—the peace—the light—the acceptance—the end—but her happiness meant more than his own—and Zach made her happy—so this was the end—the real end—the way it had to be.

'I love you,' he said.

Her eyes pressed closed. Without speaking, she leaned forward and pushed her lips to his chest, hot through the fabric of his shirt, bittersweet, the contact spearing right through to his breaking heart. Instinctively, his hand rose to cup the back of her head, waiting to tilt her face to his one last time, but she drew back and whispered. 'Don't kiss me.'

It destroyed him to step back.

It damn near killed him to watch her turn, eyes glimmering, and start to walk away.

'Please,' he found himself saying to her retreating back.

Her steps faltered. She half-turned, showing him the side of her face, keeping her unblinking gaze on the sand. 'Don't beg. I don't have the strength for that.'

The truth was in the way she swayed in the sea breeze, as if a simple gust or plea would push her into his arms.

'But I figured it out.' He stood, numb, arms by his sides. 'I figured out how we could work.'

She lifted a hand, ran it beneath her eyes. Her voice wavered as she said, 'I'm so sorry, Ethan.'

'Stevie—'

Then he saw them.

Zach's small silhouette, ghosting across the sand, shadowed by Felix. Regan stayed back, close to the bar, hands clasped beneath her chin and attention rapt on the boy as he stopped half a dozen paces from Stevie, posture tense, chin level.

As Stevie turned her back on him to walk away, Ethan didn't move, didn't speak, didn't dare to hope that his world might not quite be ending.

STEVIE HALTED, STARTLED, when Zach was suddenly in front of her. Sincerity blew his eyes wide; distress bunched his brow. Felix loomed behind him, expression serious, and Stevie had a stricken moment of déjà vu. Felix had stood with Regan when she'd returned, acting as a silent hand-holder, offering them support and the strength they lacked. And now he stood blocking Zach's escape route, as if this moment had a desired outcome, and he wasn't letting Zach backtrack until it had been achieved.

'Zach,' she said, tone dull.

He hesitated, looking over his shoulder, and Felix closed in, kneeling beside him and murmuring in his ear.

'Mum.' Zach turned to address the few paces of sand between them. 'I'm sorry I yelled at you.'

Emotionally drained and discarded, she nodded.

'Felix reminded me that you don't yell at me when you don't like what I'm doing.' His foot came out of his flip-flop, big toe digging into the sand. 'You tell me why you don't like it.'

Stevie turned her stare toward Felix. Her beautiful best friend returned her look grimly.

'And.' Zach's hands were in his pockets. 'He said I should just tell you why I don't like you and...' His eyes darted up to where Ethan stood a safe and infinitely painful distance behind her. 'Why I got upset.'

Disbelief rushed like blood to her head.

Zach was willing to talk about this.

Needing to pin the moment down, trap it right here, Stevie sat down on the spot. After a hesitation, Zach followed suit, hunching down opposite her, and Felix lowered himself behind him. They shifted, a little awkward, just the three of them, until Stevie reached out and blindly touched the sand to her right.

A moment passed, then another.

Ethan didn't join them.

His hesitation swelled the fear inside her; the fear she'd made him fall too far, and he couldn't reform his shattered hope in time to face this second chance.

Then she heard the faint squeak of footsteps in the sand, and she didn't know whether to laugh or cry when he appeared, silent, settling down beside her, head bowed, leg jiggling.

'Why did you get so upset, Zach?' Felix asked quietly.

Zach's inhale was uneven. 'Because Mum's going to love him more than me.'

Shock opened up inside her, and despair rushed in to fill the space. 'What?' Stevie reached out, grasping his knee. 'Never.'

His eyes flicked up, troubled. 'You'll want to spend more time with him than me.'

Her head was already shaking.

'It's always been just us,' he said next, pouting more than a little.

It was a few moments before she realized that this was sounding familiar. 'Zach,' she said, hand still gripping the small round of his knee. 'I feel the same way about you spending time with Ethan.'

Confused, her boy frowned at her.

'I'm scared you'll want to hang out with him more than me. That you'll want to do things with him that you and I have always done together.' Ethan sat motionless beside her, and she ached to take his hand. They were speaking about him like he wasn't there—as far as flies on the wall went, their words must be squashing him flat. 'I'm worried that you'll love him more than me. Or think he's nicer. Or funnier. Or cooler.'

Zach stared, lips parted. Then his features shifted, pulling back into a *puh-leeze* expression. 'No one's cooler than you, Mum. You're my street cred.'

She almost laughed.

Once again, Felix murmured in Zach's ear. Her boy darted a glance at Ethan, before focusing intently on a fragment of seashell. 'I mean, Ethan's cool, too, but I figured he and I would be sort of friends, you know? And Mum, you've never been jealous of my friends before.'

Friends. He wanted to be friends with Ethan. Hope moved inside her as she said, 'I'm a bit jealous of Tim.'

'Everyone's jealous of Tim.' Zach waved a hand. 'He can throw a basketball behind him and get it in the net.'

'I could teach you that,' Ethan murmured.

There was a group-wide pause.

Zach's attention fixed on him. 'Seriously?'

'Only if you want.'

'I—yeah.' The seashell held his interest again. 'I do.'

Strain stiffened Ethan's shoulders, his spine. 'Because I don't want to come between you and your mum.'

'It'd be cool if you were around, though.' Zach raised a shoulder, flashing a look at his father. Mumbling, he added, 'I'm sorry I said I didn't want to see you again. I didn't mean it.'

'Zach.' Stevie didn't want to ask and ruin this moment, but she needed to know with every beat of her pulse. 'What about me seeing Ethan again? Did you mean that?'

Her son grew still. Lips tight, his attention moved quickly between her and Ethan.

Felix nudged him in the side.

'I guess he can come over. And teach me that trick. And, sometimes, he can come over when I'm not home, too.'

Stevie's head reeled as her heart swelled, and then she was kneeling up and pulling Zach into a hug full of such relief that she didn't realize his face was squashed against her shoulder until he was pushing her away, saying, 'Mum, stop it, not in front of the guys.' But she caught his cautious smile, a new awareness that his mother's happiness was very occasionally separate from his own, and then he was caught up in a second hug, swift but sure, until Ethan released him. Zach sat back looking startled and just a little elated.

'Wow,' a woman stage-whispered behind them. 'Alexia, what *have* we missed?'

They all turned. Parker's partner Alexia stood in front of Lullabar with her best friend, Dee, returned from their girly getaway. They both wore large sunhats despite the late hour and were loaded down with luggage. Regan joined them, her attention also riveted on the scene.

'That's Ethan.' Regan's hushed voice travelled. 'He's Zach's dad. He didn't know about Zach, because Stevie thought he'd died. They've kind of fallen in love though, and Zach freaked out, but now he's just said they can be together.'

'Elevator pitch, I love it.' Dee tilted her head. 'I sense a new script idea coming on.'

Alexia murmured, 'You can't use someone's real love story for a screenplay, Dee.'

'I used mine, didn't I?'

Stevie grinned as Ethan's hand found hers. He squeezed tightly, conveying the power of his emotion in physical form, relief and awe and excitement.

They'd kind of fallen in love.

Zach had twisted around to wave. All three women

waved back, smiling delightedly.

Felix leaned back on his palms and sent Stevie a wink. She had no idea what he'd said to her son over the past few hours, but she'd never forget that he'd done it. 'Just so you know, Zach,' he said, gesturing between her and Ethan. 'These two are going to miss out on so much fun. Regan's already planning next Friday night, and I've got to say, I hope you like burgers and chips.'

Zach leapt to his feet, rounding on him in exaggerated excitement. 'I love burgers and chips. Also, I am suddenly very hungry, and I have to say hi to Dee and Alexia, and are you coming?'

Grinning, Felix rolled his eyes and pushed to his feet.

'Mum,' Zach said, pointing an urgent finger at her. 'I've got to collect more intel on this burger situation, stat. I'll meet you back here in ten.'

'Tell me what intel means.'

He pulled a face. 'Gotta go,' he said, and ran ahead of Felix.

Stevie watched the pair retreat, every other sense intent on the man beside her. The firm grip of his hand in hers, the soft sea-speckled smell of him, and the stunned undertones of his silence. She hung her head. 'I'm sorry, Ethan.'

His hand tightened. 'Why?'

'For walking away. I just—' Hadn't been able to think through the roar of devastation in her head. 'I gave you up so quickly.'

'But not easily.' He scooted in beside her, drawing her against him. 'And never again.'

She pressed her face against his chest, circling her arms around him and hugging fiercely, wanting him to feel the intensity of her need for him.

'I love you,' he said above her, not a wretched admission this time, but a precious whisper, and she twisted, seeking his mouth and kissing him, saying it back with her body, loving every part of his lips, his mouth, his face, until he was taut with energy, pushing her back into the sand. Thrilled by his grin, she softened and kissed him again, loving the press of his hands on her back, the tenderness of his mouth on hers.

'I love you, too,' she murmured against his ear. 'Now, tell me how we're going to work.'

Epilogue

IT HAD BEEN the best year of Ethan's life.

A careful start, those first few months, as they all walked the fragile ice of a new relationship, but as they ventured further on, a routine formed, solid and familiar beneath them. Ethan flew to Melbourne on Friday nights, and while Zach stayed with Felix and Regan, Ethan would watch Stevie play soccer before taking her out for a post-match dinner or drinks or live music. They spent long and luscious nights locked in each other's arms, and weekends as a new family, and inevitably, parting on Sunday nights evolved from hugs at the apartment door to avid waving at the terminal, and then worse, subdued car rides and near-silent airport goodbyes.

Returning to solitude in Sydney was eased only by Hack's delight when Ethan picked him up from the boarding kennel.

But even that came with a pang of regret, and, before long, Hack took a one-way flight to Melbourne. Ethan envied him on those lonely weeknights, imagining the boxer playing gleefully with Zach and curling up next to Stevie in his absence.

Bound by the ache of separation, Ethan and Stevie texted constantly, seeking to ease the strain of attraction over an impossible distance, the yearning to touch and talk and taste while miles apart. Nighttime phone calls rolled on for hours, voices muffled by bedsheets as they imagined their own touch as the intimate caress of the other. One such night, Stevie shared her luck at having Ethan's scent in her bed, and, soon after, began to slide one of her shirts in his bag on those muted Sunday nights. Hours later, he would drape it over his pillow, sweet with her memory.

Their weekend routine came with an expected level of disorder. Ideas and tasks could still trap Ethan in a timeless bubble, so after he missed his third Friday night flight, Daniel received a healthy pay rise as his duties broadened to book Ethan's personal flights and ensure he remembered to actually catch them.

Stevie awed him by balancing her studies along with everything else. She had a study buddy in Zach, and, surprisingly, in Regan, who'd enrolled in a horticulture course midyear. He eased the load where he could, on weekends and over the phone—although he occasionally became so absorbed in a topic that he'd chase up research papers and online texts, and she'd have to ask him to at least pretend not to understand more about her future career than she did.

As for his hyperactive tendencies, they settled on an honesty system. He didn't want grinding teeth and grating nerves. He wanted awareness. So whenever his energy sawed at their patience, they would say something like, 'How about a run, Ethan?' and he'd go vent it out, no offence taken.

A standout realization was that Zach's interest directly impacted his own. One look at his son's focused features, one excited exclamation about something in his room, and Ethan was right there with him. School projects, learning to slam-dunk backwards, cooking dinner while Stevie studied— if Zach was engaged, then Ethan was too, one hundred and ten percent.

In the depths of winter, the unhappy goodbyes became too much for them all. After a frank and well-received conversation with the design firm, Ethan's demand in the Sydney office dropped back to four days a week, and so with Zach's instant permission, he extended his stay from Friday nights to early Tuesday mornings. In theory, the weekdays in between gave Stevie and Zach time alone together, not too much change at once, but as the year yawned warmth and bright light back into their days, Zach's hugs goodbye became even tighter until one morning in early December, he said, 'I wish you could stay here all the time, Ethan.'

Moved to silence by the words he'd waited almost a year to hear, Ethan met Stevie's gaze over his son's shoulder. She was motionless in the kitchen, clutching a butter knife as if she'd stab anything that dared to try to take this moment away.

Ethan drew back, brimming with joy. 'I do, too,' he answered. 'And you know what? As of next year, I only have to be in Sydney for meetings.' And the occasional trip to Indonesia. 'But I have a new project I'm going to start working on, and I'd love to do that in Melbourne. If that's okay with you and your mum.'

Apparently, that was beyond okay, because by the time the working year ended, Ethan had officially moved in. He had a home, a family, and the love of someone who genuinely believed he was exceptional. No mistaking it.

The best year of his life.

Now, with Christmas upon them and a new tradition to uphold, they were heading back to Byron Bay for the summer. Ethan was packing from a cardboard box into a duffel bag, but he wasn't complaining.

'Mum!' Zach called from his room. 'Have you packed my iPad?'

Stevie's head snapped up from her open luggage across the bed. 'Did you tell him?'

Ethan held up his palms, smiling. 'Consider me amused but innocent.'

She ground her teeth before calling back, 'You don't have an iPad.'

There was a significant pause. 'I might have meant to say—have you packed my Christmas present?'

Stevie groaned, face palming. 'Every year,' she muttered.

Ethan grinned. 'Yeah, I've packed it,' he called. 'Preloaded with your favorite math equations. It'll be fun—no Christmas breakfast until you've solved them all.'

'No!'

'Yes!' Stevie called back, and then laid her final few shirts into the open luggage, shaking her head.

'So I was thinking.' Ethan drew his bag closed and rested it against the bed. 'Maybe when we get back, we could look for a house.'

Her gaze hit him, wide-eyed. 'A house?'

'Yeah.' He'd been hunting online for weeks. His favorite was only a few suburbs away, close to Zach's school and a tram ride to Felix and Regan's apartment. 'You know, a place with a backyard and garage and maybe even a second bathroom.'

'I—we'll have to check with Zach.'

Zach materialized in the doorway, dropping his backpack between his feet. 'I'm packed. And I shotgun the second bathroom.'

Laughing in outrage, Stevie threw a shirt at him. 'You get what you're given.'

'Which makes this shirt mine.' He held it up. 'Score, it's Björk! What do you reckon, Dad, do I hold it for ransom?'

Stunned, Ethan's heart pounded hard.

Stevie stood, suddenly motionless beside him.

Zach kicked at the carpet. 'I was thinking I could call you that sometimes, especially, you know, since...' He trailed off, gaze skirting over Stevie.

For twelve long months, Ethan had waited for this moment, and now, with nerves snaking around his middle, he knew what had prompted it. Sending Zach a secretive wink, he said, 'Of course, man.'

Zach nodded, embarrassed, and headed back to his room.

'Okay, we've got to move.' Stevie cranked the zipper closed and set her luggage on the floor. As she headed toward the door, Ethan caught up her hand and tugged her around to face him. A dry smile lifted her lips as she said, 'We're kind of running late.'

'He wants to call me dad.'

Her grip tightened briefly as she smiled. 'I know.'

'And I want you to call me your husband.'

She blinked, shocked, her hand going slack in his.

Locking nerves down with a deep breath, Ethan drew a small box from his pocket. He heard Stevie's breath catch as he opened it, felt his own move ragged in his lungs as he revealed a simple silver band. 'Will you marry me, Stevie?'

She stared at the ring.

'I'm hoping you'll say yes,' he murmured, praying this wasn't too much, too soon.

She snuck a glance up at him, wonder sparkling in her clever brown eyes. 'I'm not wearing a dress.'

'I'm not asking a woman who wears dresses to marry me.'

She hesitated, overwhelmed. 'I want Regan as my

bridesmaid and Felix as my best man.'

His lips curved, and he brushed his thumb over her knuckles. 'I couldn't imagine a more fitting bridal party.'

'I want Zach to stand with us.'

'Where else would he stand?'

Clearly touched, she inched toward him. 'I want the ceremony to be small. Casual.'

He tugged her all the way against him, running his cheek down the side of her face. His mouth hovered over hers as he said, 'I want you to say yes.'

At that, she grinned, and every thought in his head fell silent until nothing but this woman existed, brave and tender and true.

And his whole world said, 'Yes.'

The End

Acknowledgements

Thank you to my support team. Dom, Mum, and Grace: you're my calming cup of three.

Thanks to Tule Publishing for giving me the time to get this right, and Sinclair, for your encouragement.

As always, thank you to my critique group for saying it like it is. You make my stories stronger.

I delved into many TED talks and blogs on adults living with ADHD. Huge shout out to those who shared their experiences. Much appreciation also goes to the website shitmy6yearoldsays.wordpress.com, for inspiring Zach (look it up, that kid's a cracker).

And to my readers, you're the light at the end of the writing tunnel.

xx

If you enjoyed *Breaking Good*,
check out more titles by Madeline Ash

Book 1: *The Playboy*

Book 2: *Her Secret Prince*
2016 RITA® nominated

Book 3: *You for Christmas*

Book 4: *Breaking Good*

Available now at your favorite online retailer!

About the Author

Madeline has always lived in Melbourne. She is emotionally allergic to spontaneity, and yet doesn't mind the weather that drags her into rain when she's planned for sunshine. She likes to call this her wild side.

She's a Virgo, vegetarian, and once had a romantic suspense-style dream in which the hero was a shredded lettuce sandwich and the villain was a cherry tomato. The tomato got away. She took the dream as a sign that she'd better stick to writing contemporary romance.

Her stories have spunky heroines, strong heroes, and as much dialogue as she can cram in. As for why she writes romance, she's in a long-term relationship with the genre and writing such stories makes it happy.

Visit her website at MadelineAsh.net

Thank you for reading

Breaking Good

If you enjoyed this book, you can find more from all our great authors at TulePublishing.com, or from your favorite online retailer.

TULE
PUBLISHING

Printed in Australia
AUOC02n0000210817
288747AU00004B/7/P